Night Side
of
Nature

James K. Pratt

NIGHT SIDE OF NATURE

Copyright © 2017 James K. Pratt

First Edition-May 2017

V 1.58 (Based on Kindle v.13)

All Rights Reserved

ACKNOWLEDGMENTS

Special thanks to my father, Kyle Pratt, and to everyone who reviewed my first two books.

Part I: The New Girl

1. THE NEW GIRL

I'd hate to be the new girl at school, especially during the middle of the school year. So many eyes spying on you, and you know it. Worse, you overthink everything you do. We rarely saw newbies. This was a private school, an expensive one at that, near the 'burbs of Seattle.

"Who is she?" I asked, looking at the tall brunette. She stood two heads taller than me, and wore a dress in a style I'd not seen. I wondered where she got it. "Has she been here before? She looks familiar." I couldn't kick the feeling that I'd seen her before.

Anne, who sat beside me on a schoolyard bench shrugged. "Oh, the new girl? I don't know her name. I saw her first this Tuesday. Avoid her, she's weird. I've been told she walks to school."

"Walks?"

"Yeah, weird right?" Anne asked.

The school is in the middle of nowhere with two miles of old forest in every direction. She looked old enough to drive, too. At least she looked that way. Sometimes you can't tell.

"Quiet type too," Anne said, "Oh, now she's looking at you... she's coming this way."

Anne went to her phone. I tried to look normal, like I wasn't talking about the girl walking toward us. I don't think I pulled it off.

"Hey, maybe you can help me. I'm new around here," the new girl said.

Oddly, while she stood over me and I sat there on the bench, I had a strong sense of déjà-vu, like I had met her long ago.....

"I'm Rachel," said the new girl.

"Funny, that's my sister's name. I'm Alexia." She kind of looked like my sister. I'd not seen her in forever.

Rachel tilted her head, "Could you help me find where my next class is?" she asked, showing me her class schedule.

"So let's see, ah, I'm taking the same class. Come with me."

The bell rang. Break time was over.

Perhaps I should ask her questions—more to gossip about with my friends. Or maybe I should invite her to my friend's party tonight. Invite an outsider to the vicious cliques of prep school? I shook the thought from my head. *I'm not that mean, am I?*

"Where are you from?" I asked.

"Vancouver."

"Oh, next to Portland? I love Portland." That was a lie. *Its only claim to fame is Powell's Bookstore and who wants old books these days besides old people... and Portland has hipsters, lots of them.*

"No. Vancouver, B.C.," she corrected.

"Wow, I always wanted to go." For some reason my mother hated the place, and never lets me go there. *No, really, she actually sat me down one day and made me promise not to go there... for no particular reason.*

When we got to class, Rachel sat in front of me. I felt like she did it on purpose. No one normally sat there anyway; it was right in front of the teacher's desk.

Mr. Dell lectured on a piece of art. It was something trite – a picture of a man putting on a mask. "So," the teacher said, "What, if anything, is the artist trying to say?"

Rachel raised her hand. "Well, if you wanted to spin it into something more than a painting of a guy with a mask, then maybe... everyone has a dark side."

"Good. I agree," the teacher smiled, "I think the masked man is showing a universal truth—that we hide our negative side behind a mask."

"But actually, I think it's a tiny bit of truth wrapped up in a lie," Rachel said.

The class giggled. *Being weird on the first day, not a smart play.*

"So are you saying we don't have a dark side?" asked the teacher.

"No, I'm saying most of the time our so called 'dark side' is really just positive traits that society looks down on. Traits that have potentially good uses."

Whatever does that mean?

The teacher chuckled, "Alright, perhaps a little more philosophical than I was looking for."

The rest of the class session went on without her saying anything.

After class, Anne caught up with me looking very serious. "I know what you're thinking, you want to talk to Rachel and get some gossip. Sit this one out," Anne said, talking to me quietly in the hallway.

What? "Sit this one out?" *When did she ever say that? And why do I see concern in her eyes?*

"She's the new girl. I want to see what she's like." As I trotted off, I felt Anne's eyes on me. I looked back. Her expression appeared nervous and a bit angry. I didn't understand but wasn't going to turn around and figure it out. Anne never acted weird like that. It must be that she just doesn't like her for some reason.

To be honest, gossip during the last few weeks had been getting rather dry since rumors about what was really found in the Biology teacher's desk started to die down.

"So," I hurried down the hall to catch up with Rachel, "You made art class more interesting."

"I know," she smiled. "What a big dork I was. Teachers love cookie-cutter answers, and I like to turn things up a notch. Besides, it's fun to mess with them; most aren't very bright."

"You really think that?" I didn't, though part of me wanted to like her anyway for killing the daily bloviation of art class.

"Come on, if they were really smart would they be trying to herd knowledge into the brains of little brats for a living?"

Cynical, cynical. And oddly enough, she sounded older than her age, especially with that "little brats" comment.

"You disagree?" Rachel asked. We walked out of the building heading toward the parking lot.

"Meh." I shrugged.

"Very well, stay on the fence then. See you soon. Gotta go."

"Go? How did you get here?" We had walked past the parking lot and stood at the point where the parking lot became the road.

"I walked."

"How? There isn't anything but trees for miles?"

She shrugged.

"I can give you a ride."

"No thanks."

Before she left, I wanted to address that nagging feeling. "I think I've seen you before," I said to her as she walked away.

"We've met," she looked over her shoulder with a smirk.

"Really, when?"

"Not sure," she said, still smirking. Then she chuckled and added, "Got the same feeling when I saw you this morning. It'll come to you."

If she wanted to be mysterious that was fine. Too often, people who like to be mysterious normally have nothing to share. Maybe her ride was down the road or something. For now, I decided to forget about it.

When I got back home from school, I looked for my sister Cordelia right away. Friends are one thing, but siblings are much more important. When I left the garage and entered the house, I knew she wasn't in her room; her door was open. It was always closed when she was inside. Pieces of ripped paper and a hair band spilled past the threshold of her door and invaded the hallway. Cordelia's room was always a mess. *The nice maid must hate her bedroom.* I looked for my sister in the kitchen. Stepping down into the living room, I saw her at the kitchen table drawing a picture. She drew a man standing outside a burning house.

My sister was a freshman, so school ended sooner for her. One of what Mother referred to as 'the help' picked up Cordelia after school. She looked sad and made no eye contact. When Cordelia's sad, she wants to be alone, but talking usually made her feel better.

"How was your day?" I asked.

Cordelia shrugged, feigning apathy, another bad sign. I always liked to talk her out of these moods. *It's no good to deal with sadness alone.*

"What's wrong?"

"Mom left her wing of the house, she's in a bad mood."

Mother seldom left her wing of the mansion. But her bad moods were nothing new. *There's something more going on here.*

"What did she do?"

She shook her head, still not looking at me as she drew her picture.

"It's not your fault. We both know we're better people than 'mommy dearest.'"

She chuckled at the mommy dearest comment. "You got that right." Now Cordelia relented a bit and gave me brief eye contact.

"There's no reason for our mother to be mean. We've got to keep telling ourselves that."

She looked up and held my gaze. "She said I raided her liquor cabinet."

Mother hated when things went missing.

"Yeah, right. You'd never do that?" I knew she didn't.

She raised her eyebrows and said, "Not normally."

Stealing liquor isn't like Cordelia. There is a party tonight. Was she invited to the party, too?

When I left Cordelia, she felt better. I would return to her later. Wanting to see pictures of better days, I went to my room and got my picture album out.

I didn't have a bookshelf in my room, not with eBook readers and all. My picture album was in my walk-in closet. There, I had 40 pairs of pants, 60 dresses, 80 tops, and 60 pairs of shoes. Yes, I counted. My closet was the size of many people's living rooms. In the back of the closet, I found several yearbooks and a large old-fashioned scrapbook with loads of pictures. On the first page were pictures of my dad; they were taken around the time of my birth. Mother never spoke of him.

I walked out of my closet and closed the door

behind me with my foot. Sitting on the bed cross-legged, I turned the pages of my scrapbook and gasped. A picture of my sister Rachel! She looked just like the "Rachel" I met today. In the 13-year-old pic, she passed me a present from beside the Christmas tree. The picture was taken two weeks before she disappeared.

2. A PICTURE OF A MISSING SISTER

I gazed at the picture of my sister in my tattered scrapbook. *What's going on? Why does this new girl Rachel look exactly like my sister and have her same name?*

Now I was angry. *Is this "Rachel thing" a joke, an elaborate prank? If so, by who and why?* Then I did what any girl would do, I turned to my phone for help.

I snapped a picture of Rachel in my album and sent it to Anne with the message, "Look familiar?"

Anne didn't text back. *She's a little old-fashioned. She uses phones like they are only phones, weird huh?*

"I'm confused," Anne said over the phone. "That's an old picture." I heard the familiar sound of her pulling a record sleeve off a shelf. I've never understood my generation's fascination with old technology.

"That's my sister, Rachel."

Anne gasped and paused. "Don't tell anyone about this. I'll come over, okay?"

"Why? Can't you see this is some kind of joke? And why don't I come over to your house for a change?"

"Yeah, as soon as my parents stop being weird."

One odd thing about Anne… I've never been to her house. She never lets me visit. I've always wondered what her house was like. I imagined it looked goody-goody like a gingerbread house, but filled with crazy people, by the way she described her mother being on Valium all the time.

Before she hung up, I had to ask, "And why not tell someone?"

"Because people will think you're *crazy*."

"No they won't."

"Alexia, don't risk it. I'm coming over. Don't do anything until then."

Anne and I were sitting in my bedroom. We failed to find Rachel on any social network, though we searched the Vancouver, B.C. area for anyone by that name. I suggested she might have deleted her account. *A person without a social media presence, that didn't seem right.*

"This is weird, when you see her at school next, avoid her," Anne suggested.

This situation felt so peculiar it proved hard to

ignore. I really didn't want to avoid her. "No way, I want answers."

Anne's eyes narrowed; for some reason, she seemed angry with me. Her eyes said, "No."

"What's wrong with getting answers?" I asked.

Anne was slender and always liked to be moving, so she paced while I sat on my bed.

"No one will listen to us because we are teenagers," she said. "Your mom doesn't listen to you. My parents ignore me. I've read about ghosts on the internet. They show up at school looking like dead friends or, in your case, a long lost sister, and soon after that friends of the dead person disappear."

"Cute Anne, creepypasta is the best you can do. News flash... ghosts don't apply to prep school!"

Anne closed her eyes and held up her hands "It sounds crazy, but so is the situation you're in."

"It's impossible to look just like someone."

Anne interrupted. "This isn't a practical joke. No one signs up for school to play a joke. The school wouldn't mess around, and your mother doesn't have a sense of humor from what I know."

She's right, and no one avoids aging for fifteen years.

Anne continued, "When you've eliminated the impossible, what remains—however unlikely—must be the truth. So, if not a ghost, something not natural."

Quoting Sherlock. Cute.

Her advice seemed to make sense. Yet, for the first time, I worried. I felt guilty for giving in to childhood fears of ghosts. *There's nothing lurking in the dark; just a strange girl who looks like my sister.*

Then it came back to me how she smiled when I said I'd seen her before, and she concurred. She also smiled when I pointed out she had the same name. Could she be my sister, still 18 and alive?

Anne excused herself to go to the bathroom.

I got a call. My phone read: "unknown number."

"Hello?"

"It's me. Rachel. I don't have much time. Just listen. Is Anne with you?"

"She went to the bathroom."

"Go to the balcony."

I stepped out and looked at the pool directly below. Beyond that the garden, wrapped with a fifteen-foot tall brick fence topped with shards of glass. I wondered why mom wanted the place to be a fort.

"I *am* your sister," Rachel said on the phone, "but more importantly, did you find the key and letter I hid for you years ago?"

My heart rapped in my chest. *Yes I did.* My sister left a letter hidden in the spine of my favorite book, *Peter and Wendy.*

"Are you there?" Rachel raised her voice a little when I didn't answer.

"Yes." I said.

"So you found the key?"

"Yeah."

"Is Anne still gone?" Rachel asked.

I heard a flush. "She is. Will you tell me what's going on?"

"Soon. Anne is working for our mother. For now, you need to pretend like nothing's wrong, and things will be fine," Rachel said.

Anne opened the door of the balcony.

Rachel's tone changed to happy-go-lucky. "I'm sure I'll see you at the party, bye." She hung up. Her shift in tone seemed strange, but then I considered the fact that she might have heard Anne coming in and changed her tone of voice as a cover.

"That was my fake sister," I said.

She tilted her head. "You okay? You look pale."

"I'm fine," I said. *Anne is working for my mom?*

"What did she say?"

I quickly figured a lie. "Nothing, just asking what to wear to the party."

"Don't let what I said worry you. This will go away soon enough." She looked hard at me. "I better go. I gotta get dressed for the party."

I sighed, now alone in my room. I probably should have seen Anne out, but instead, I sat there, wondering how this little bit of weirdness got so big.

3. PARTY

I knocked on Lionel's door. His family's mansion was surrounded by old evergreen trees. No neighbors for a quarter mile. That was a good thing, too, because the music blasted, and I felt the vibration of the bass through the heavy wooden doors. I knocked on the door again figuring no one heard me.

A boy who looked like Harry Potter greeted me. He wore jeans and a red t-shirt topped off with round glasses. Just Felix, Lionel's younger brother.

"Hello." I stepped in. "Where's Lionel?"

Felix pointed into the living room. Lionel stood in the middle of a dozen people, all smiling and laughing, each with red cups in their hands.

Stopping by the kitchen, I dropped off beer that I'd bought on the way. I felt glad I looked older and owned a fake ID.

"Aha," I said, spying expensive alcohol. *So my sister is here, and she did raid Mom's liquor cabinet.* I looked to the living room for my sister. *Yes, there she is. Confrontation time.*

"Cordelia, what are you doing here?" I asked.

"What do you mean?" Cordelia scowled. "You're here."

"This party's too old for you." I instantly regretted my words.

"Well, I see you brought beer, so you're not telling Mom." Cordelia turned with a scowl and vanished into the den.

I wouldn't have told Mom anyway.

Lionel walked up. "Hey, your sister out did you as far as drinks go."

"Yeah, Mother's not happy, but she needs to drink less, anyway."

"Whoa, she *stole* from your mother?"

"Yes..." Before I finished talking, a pair of girls swept him away, leaving me alone.

Part of me liked Cordelia for stealing from Mom, yet I didn't want Mother to have any righteous anger against us.

A pair of hands slid over my eyes, "Guess who?" said a familiar voice.

The one I had been avoiding – my boyfriend, Jonathan. I forced a smile to make my voice sound happy. *I wish I could be happy.* "Hmm, a cheerleader?"

He chuckled "No."

He's nice. Maybe that's been the problem. Jonathan is a gentleman, and I'm really not nice.

"Okay, second guess." *I gotta make this a good one.* "My swim coach?"

"Yuck! No!"

"Oh, Jonathan." His hands vanished. I turned around to see him smiling. "Well, I was close with swim coach."

He laughed with a real smile. I had to put on mine. The fact that he's nice made it harder to break up with him. I didn't want to do it tonight.

I glanced over his shoulder, hoping to see someone I could drag in between us. Instead, I spotted Rachel on the second floor, standing by the railing. She was talking to someone and didn't see me.

"What's wrong?" Jonathan asked.

"Look, you see that girl up there?"

"The new girl?" Jonathan asked.

"Yeah, she looks just like my sister."

He looked confused, then I saw the realization set

in, "Oh, you mean your *older* sister, the missing one?"

"Yeah, she has the same name and appearance."

I told him the whole story. Well, not the part where Rachel claimed Anne is working for my mother. That's too weird. The thing about Jonathan, he listens. Sometimes I wondered why I wanted to break up with him. Especially since Lionel, whom I like more, can space out. Sometimes I think I like the wrong people to hurt myself or something.

Jonathan shook his head. "Stop worrying and ask this 'Rachel' what she wants, where she's been, and why she's back now."

"But Anne said—"

"Look, Anne is wrong. Ask Rachel. What is clear is that you know nothing now, and it costs you next to nothing to ask." He looked into my eyes. "I see you are afraid, but knowing more will fix that. Something *is* going on. It's all just too weird. She can't be your sister because she hasn't aged. My guess...something strange is going on."

That's Jonathan, in just minutes he clears up my problem. It was good advice, and I'll take it.

Before I reached my "sister" Rachel, Cordelia crossed my path. Her narrow eyes told me she was still angry. She had a right to be mad, but I didn't want her at a party with people drinking. *Yet, I'm here, and I'm not much older than her. I treated her like a child when she's not. She's a teenager like me.*

I stopped my sis. "Cordelia, I'm sorry. I'm glad you're here." I tried to believe it too, but the thought of her possibly getting drunk bothered me. *Hypocrite, you brought the beer.*

Cordelia didn't say anything. *That's her way of saying I need to say more.*

"You're my sister, so I worry. I'm sorry. I overreacted."

She smiled. We're close. We needed to be, with Mother being who she was and all. The two of us were the only family we had. We parted on good terms, but I would be looking out to see that she's okay.

Before I crossed the room to Rachel, Anne got in the way. She stood by the couch with Lionel just inches away, flirting with a girl. A few bottles lay empty on the table before them. Based on the inane conversation between Lionel and the girl, they seemed to have passed being buzzed, and slid into slightly stupid drunk.

"Ignore Rachel," Anne said, "Whatever this is, it will go away."

Anne is acting so weird, what gives? "I want good answers."

Anne nodded to something over my shoulder. "Cordelia is in trouble."

Laughter roared by the pool outside. I turned

around. A varsity football player grabbed my sister's breast. I thought about getting Lionel to do something. But anger burned the sane thoughts away.

No, I will do something myself.

Cordelia shoved the big guy, but the jock hardly budged. He wore a stupid grin on his face like he was proud of himself.

Murder time! I snatched one of Lionel's beer bottles and marched towards the man.

Lionel called out. "I'm still drinking that ...okay, do what you want... love you!" *He said it while drunk, so the "love you" comment doesn't count.*

I trotted over to the pool. Lionel's pool looked nice, though it was only half the size of the one in my backyard.

I smashed the bottle over the jock's head. Glass and beer ran down his nose. He lunged at me, but I rammed the heel of my hand into his nose. Grabbing him by the throat, I shoved him. The jock stumbled backwards into the pool.

Splash.

Not amazed? I did it wearing a tight red dress and high-heels; show some respect.

Partiers clapped. One of my high heels broke off my shoe, so I threw them both at the dumb jock in the pool. His fat face reddened with anger and a lot of blood lathered the crown of his head and nose. Testosterone and rage filled his eyes.

"Will you gentlemen please get him out of here," I said.

"No problem, Alexia," said Richard Attucks, one of the guys from school.

I marched off barefoot.

With the fight and the mook's social standing over, I headed back inside. My sister looked surprised and maybe a little grateful.

Lionel held his third beer. "Am I drunk, or did you beat up a football player?"

"No, you're drunk, *and* I beat up a football player," I said.

Beating up a jock who weighed almost twice as much as me didn't make sense. *I weigh about 132, and I never fight. I'm not that strong, nor am I ever that graceful in high heels. Who is, anyway? I mean, besides a masochist? Maybe I'm just lucky.*

Now, where was I before I got myself distracted? Oh, yeah, my "sister" Rachel.

She stood by the stairs looking at me. *Then again, after the fight who wasn't looking at me?*

"Let's talk." I followed her into a guest room. We were alone. "Here try this." She snatched a red plastic cup from the top of a dresser.

I normally say no to strange drinks, but it smelled good. Really good. I took the cup and chugged it down. It had alcohol with something else that tasted iron-like. "Wow, what was that?"

Her eyebrow raised, "Whoa, greedy much?"

I looked at the cup, now empty. That went fast. "You said you were my sister. How is that possible?"

Her expression changed to something harder, "I *am* your sister. Right now you only think Mom is evil." Her tone was dead serious, but she didn't answer my question.

If she wanted to hype this, I'm leaving. I headed for the door.

She continued. "I ran away from home with some cousins of Lionel and Felix. There were five of us. Were anyway; I might be the last."

I didn't ask about her possibly being the last. I didn't want to know. She ran away? Why? I wanted to ask, but I didn't. I wanted to know why she didn't age. She hadn't explained that, so I didn't care about anything else. *If she can't explain why she still looks like Rachel the day she left, then this is just a joke, a bad one at that.*

Furthermore, Mom's a bitch, and I hate her sometimes; but she isn't truly evil, just a pathetic, selfish person. I have to admit my sister is gone. Not gone. Dead. What kind of sister has no contact for over a decade? She's not standing before me. I have to stop this, or I'll be a joke. "Get lost, whoever you are." I walked to the door.

Rachel stood there at lightning speed. "Please don't go. You wouldn't believe why I haven't aged if I told you. You need to hear it from our mother and Anne. Can you get to Mom's side of the mansion?"

"Yeah."

"Anne meets with Mother every Friday at exactly three."

"No she's doesn't. She's just getting off from school."

"A.M."

"A.M.? Talking about what? That makes no sense." *She told me her parents made her go to bed early.*

Rachel, shrugged still standing by the door. "About you, I guess."

"Why?"

"As best I can tell, Mother always hired a friend to look after us. Our sister has one, too. If you can find a way to listen to Mother and Anne talk, then you'll believe."

I just stood there, not sure what to say. *If I listened, I'd believe. Fine.*

She continued. "Text me afterward." She gave me a phone. "Use only the phone network, not our home's wireless net. And I'm sure your regular phone is bugged."

Hired "Friends?" Bugged cell phones? Now I wanted her to be wrong. I remembered the key I found in the *Peter and Wendy* book. "What about the key I found?"

"Later." Rachel said, opening the window. Then she climbed and fell through. I darted to the window to see if she was okay. She was running into the woods. The fall didn't appear to have slowed her down. She charged into the night like an Olympic sprinter.

So, if she's right, I'm going to be a believer in a few hours. My best friend has betrayed me. But why? What is going on?

If my life will never be the same, so be it.

4. I BELIEVE

That morning, I didn't sleep. My head swam with the mystery of a sister who shouldn't be my age and the possibility that my best friend was a backstabber. And my mom... well, I didn't know what to think about her.

I needed to wait until 3:00 A.M. to overhear this meeting in Mom's office with Anne. I filled the early morning hours on my phone, reading people's posts, and playing games.

One thing haunted my mind, making my thoughts run in circles. Anne is supposedly working with Mother. My own best friend was in on this. Whatever *this* meant. *What are they up to?* That remained the loneliest thought of all. I had many friends, but only *one* best friend. *So, if Anne has betrayed me, and I'm breaking up with Jonathan, then I'd be... alone. Friends are my world.*

My alarm clock said 2:50 A.M. I better get going and see if Rachel is right.

A few minutes later, I opened the only door to Mother's wing of the house. Her part of the mansion was quiet.

Her personal bodyguards would be walking about, so I needed to be careful.

Having bodyguards is overkill, if you ask me. She must have enemies though, because I've even wanted to kill her. Those feelings for her started at age four. Oh, to be young and not so innocent.

I walked in, careful to be quiet, yet mindful not to appear like I was sneaking.

"Ma'am?" A man's voice asked.

I spun around with fear shooting up my spine. *Caught so quickly.* One of Mother's men stood before me. I knew him as the head of Mother's bodyguards. He looked cute in a bland, male-model sort of way.

"Yes?" I asked.

"This side of the house is restricted," said Cute Guard.

"Since when?" I looked him straight in the eye. My reward was seeing a bit of discomfort, perhaps my first sign that things were not right. My sister and I were allowed here if we stay out of everyone's way. "Look, I just want to go to the bathroom. Mine doesn't work." *Note: sabotage the toilet.*

"Very well," he said, "I will wait outside and see

that you leave."

"Creep off, perv!"

He looked uncomfortable and then finally said, "Leave as soon as possible. This side is restricted."

"Right." *I hoped Rachel was lying, but the way the bodyguard is acting makes me think she's telling the truth.*

I went into the bathroom nearest her office and locked the door. I sat on the toilet lid. To my surprise, I heard Mother talking. Her voice came through the bathroom fan. *The vents to her office and the bathroom must be connected. She's up late.* But I always knew she worked odd hours. There was another voice with her in the office— Anne's!

"How long do I have to keep doing this?" Anne asked.

"Until graduation, after that I shouldn't need you anymore," Mother said.

"I'm in danger. Alexia is violent. She took down a football player in four seconds tonight. She's turning."

Turning? What are you talking about? How am I a danger to Anne?

"We're all violent, you know that, but you are older than her, and Alexia hasn't turned yet. So, stop complaining. Keep to your duties, they're more important now. Tell me more about my daughter's reaction to seeing my wayward Rachel."

So Rachel is my sister.

I heard someone walk down the hall to Mother's office door.

"I said no interruptions." She never liked being distracted. She once smacked me across the face when I was six; I just wanted to show her that I got an 'A' on my spelling test.

A male voice whispered, then heavy footsteps left the office.

"Alexia is here in my half of the mansion," Mother said. "You will need to stay here until she leaves. Now where did we leave off?"

"As I said on the phone, your daughter is having trouble coming to terms with her sister's visit. She knows something odd is afoot and will act rashly. I just don't know how."

"Afoot," and "rashly?" Since when did Anne talk like that?

Mother's tone was even. "Rachel legally left my house, and she didn't return here alone, so don't move against her. She is protected by another House."

Rachel didn't come alone? She said her friends who ran away with her were dead. Therefore, those she came with are not her runaway friends. When Mother says leave them alone, that means they are powerful friends. Mother isn't tolerant of defiance. Could these people helping Rachel have shown an interest in her grudge against Mother? Rachel never mentioned anyone else with her. I will need to see if Rachel brings them up. That way I can see if she's being completely honest.

Something else is wrong, more than Anne meeting with Mother. Something else wasn't being discussed, something both Mother and Anne knew but didn't mention. There simply is no need to say it. What is it? Rachel knows, and she said I wouldn't believe her.

Mother spoke again. "You will keep an eye on my daughter until she graduates. Come up with a story for why you disappear afterwards, if you like. I don't care."

Neither of them really cared for me. What had I done to deserve this? I'm a good person. I'm a good sister and a good friend. What have I done to be completely alone? My mother treats me like a possession needing to be watched. My best friend is a complete fraud.

I vacated that wing of the house and saw only the bodyguard at the door. No doubt ensuring that I left.

Determined not to cry until I hit my bed, I ran to it quickly. I wanted to wake up from this nightmare, hug my sister, and tell her I love her.

The worst part is, I didn't yet know how much of my life is a lie or what I am "turning" into.

Wiping away a tear as I sat on the edge of my bed, I texted Rachel using the phone she gave me at the party...

"I BELIEVE."

5. SLEEPLESS NIGHTS

A war spun in my head. What I learned kept me from sleeping. I wanted to hate Anne, and a second later forgive her.

At 7:00 A.M., after sabotaging my toilet, I decided to skip school and went to the public library.

I knew things were bad when I skipped school for a place even *more* boring.

Books are great, but libraries suck. These places smell musty, and they're full of books that are seldom touched. Plus, the person sitting on a sofa in the main reading area is a pedophile. I've seen his picture at school. Also, drug paraphernalia has been found in the bathrooms. Welcome to your public library, a shithole.

I took a computer terminal and started a new email account. Last night, Rachel texted me back that I shouldn't use the phone too much from home. Data traffic might be monitored from my house. She said I should start an email account at a library. I texted that I don't like libraries, and she said, "Good, no one will look for you there." She added, "Just say you're doing homework if anyone asks."

With my account set up, I typed, *"What now?"* I clicked send.

My email account showed I received a message. Rachel wrote back. *"Mother's lackeys are out looking for you. Leave your car and get a ride out of town. Go to a place with lots of people."*

I wrote back, *"How do you know that?"*

She replied, *"I know Mother."*

I got a cab to the mall thirty minutes away. It was public enough for now. I stopped at one of the mall's restrooms.

As I washed my hands, a woman in her mid-twenties came by. "Oh, wow. When did you turn?"

Turn? That word again. What does that mean? I should have asked Rachel by email. Great, just play along. "Recently." I forced a smile.

She nods. "I've gotta see your mother. That time of year again."

I have no idea what you're talking about. "Yeah, yeah," I said, trying to sound confident. Then she left, leaving me clueless.

If I did "turn," how did she know? Smell? I looked in the mirror. I don't look different. Just tired. What does it even mean? And how did she know my mother? If I did "turn," how did this happen? I might have asked, "What did I get myself into," but that wasn't the right question. What was I born into?

I went to a coffee shop and used the phone Rachel gave me to text her.

Me: Someone just told me I was turned.

Rachel: You are not turned; but without your choosing, you are changing.

Me: What's going on?

Rachel: I'm your sister, you need to trust me. Don't worry. What's happening is that your body is changing. Right now, you have a choice, return to your mother or meet me.

Those are my only options? I want to think of a third because I don't like either of them. One of the best things my mother taught me was, "when people say you have two bad choices, it's because they don't want you to consider a third and better one."

Me: You've given me no reason to think you are any better.

She'll write back. Bingo, she did.

Rachel: I'm risking my life to help you. You remember the restaurant we went to on our last Christmas?

How could I forget our last Christmas?

Me: Yes.

Rachel: We meet there… in 30 minutes.

6. THE LAST CHRISTMAS

The last Christmas season with my eldest sister Rachel, we both hoped our mother might show a softer side with Cordelia on the way. I was four years old during the Christmas season before Rachel vanished. Mother was not bearing my unborn sister Cordelia. Someone else was doing that, so I had to learn a new word, "surrogate." I was confused about why Mother couldn't have kids like the Moms of some of my friends. Later, since Mother doesn't like kids, I wondered why she was having a third one, anyway?

Rachel took me Christmas shopping at the mall. After that, she took me to a restaurant a few blocks away. I ordered hot chocolate with whipped cream on top. I loved it. Drinking it, I felt like the winter cold and snow melted right off me. Looking back, when I was older, I understood that my sister was more of a mother to me than our own.

After Rachel disappeared, I never mentioned the restaurant to anyone. I wanted the restaurant to be me and my sister's place. When I was 13 years old, I returned. Along with school, it was one of the few places with good memories. I went there to sort out my feelings, to pray, to be sad, to hide for a while, and to stay away from home.

Rachel ran away for a reason. Meeting her meant I was meeting someone who actively defied my mother. This meant trouble if I was caught. Rachel's running away meant Mother couldn't control her, and Mother hated people who defied her.

"Hey Sis," Rachel popped into a seat across from me.

"Hi. If you are my sister, where have you been all these years?"

"Hiding. Trying to live out of the shadow of our mother, Fiona. She's more than just a rich businesswoman. She is *powerful*."

"What kind of power? Does that connect with my best friend spying on me and you not aging?"

"Listen, the reason Mother is powerful is that she isn't human. Neither is our sister, Anne, Lionel, Felix, or me. Nor are you, Alexia. That's why our mother has always needed surrogates to have children."

Many of the people close to me aren't human? "What are we?"

"We are a people who have lived alongside

humanity for about 2,000 years. You're a vampire."

Oh, like hell I am. "Excuse me? I'm not a vampire. I don't drink blood."

"Well, you're not *exactly* a vampire; you're a half-vampire. Part of you is human, but your DNA from our mother will take over. Vampires can't have children, but they are close snapshots of what they were in human life. Human eggs remain, but they have vampire DNA. That's why vampires have children by surrogates."

The waiter poured us water. We each thanked him.

"Don't vampires burn in the sun?" I asked. "I've seen you outside in the day."

"Aww, you need to read more books. I thought I taught you better, by reading to you every night. The sensitivity to sunlight is an invention of the movies. The German movie *Nosferatu* made the idea of vampires burning in daylight popular. Real vampires can walk in daylight just fine. And it's a stupid weakness when you think about it. We're not magic."

"So, um, you're not... dead?" I asked, taking my glass.

"No, I'm not undead. But we are stronger than normal humans. We don't seem to age... but bullets can kill us."

"So you die like normal humans."

She tilted her head, "*Well*, we are harder to kill."

"Okay, where do vampires come from?"

"Romans thought that drinking the blood of dead gladiators made them stronger. Well, they were sort of right, because one of them drank *a lot* of blood and became the first vampire. And if you're wondering, vampires haven't been able to reproduce that in other humans. So, the first human to become a vampire was a very *odd* one. Oh, and your grandmother is Elizabeth Bathory."

"Eww." *One of history's most prolific serial killers. That's bad. I read her Wikipedia page because she had the same last name as me. On the bright side, I have royal blood. Cool.* "If vampires are immortal and have been around for 2,000 years, why don't vampires take over the world? There must be lots of us."

The waiter asked us if we were ready to order. I said we'd decide in a minute. After he left, we continued to talk.

"Vampires have never been strong in numbers. We are also a divided people fighting among ourselves. And vampires can't just bite anyone and turn them. Often, early in a vampire's new life, like within a year, we have an urge to drink lots of blood, human blood. It'll drive you crazy. After drinking human blood, you'll have an urge to bite a human so that you turn them. This will happen again maybe every 50 or 100 years. It's the only time we can turn someone."

I pretended to look at the menu but couldn't read it, this was too distracting. "So you're saying when I turn, I'm going to want to kill a human and then turn another?"

"Yes."

"How do we stop that?"

"I'll watch you until the feeling passes; you'll be fine."

"So when will I become a vampire?"

"Maybe in months, or even days. You'll turn, and it will be sudden. At the latest, you'll turn at 21 years of age."

"So when you say my mother is powerful you mean—"

"You're a royal," Rachel said.

I'm vampire royalty. Wow. My head filled with questions. But one thing bothered me, and I had to ask. "Will it hurt? Turning I mean." My heart stopped at the sight of Anne walking up to our table.

"Well," Anne took a seat and smiled coolly, "Glad I found you guys."

Both Rachel and I were speechless. *Rachel ran away and Mother hates her, even if she doesn't ever mention her. Now, I have been seen meeting with Rachel behind Mother's back. Would I lose Rachel just when she came back? How much trouble was I in? Could I fix this?*

"Hello, Alexia," Anne said to me, "Come with me. We need to talk." Then, Anne said to Rachel, "Fiona says you need to leave town. I suggest you do so."

As she walked toward the exit, Rachel texted me, *"Go with her. We'll meet again."*

7. FIONA BATHORY

I rode in Anne's car. Anne tried to talk to me, but I ignored her. She still tried to pretend to be my friend.

I entered the living room on Mother's side of the house. Yes, we had two living rooms. No, it doesn't make sense. Lights were off. Fireplace lit. Mother sat on a wooden chair, which I imagined to be a throne. That's how she sat in it. Now that I knew her to be a vampire, I wondered if she kept her side of the house old-fashioned as a comfort thing.

"What has she told you?" Mother asked. *She knows little about what happened. She's trying to gauge the situation.*

"Rachel said you were *evil* and told me I needed to run off with her. She said that you are a vampire."

Mother was silent. It was unlike her. "That is true. But more importantly, she ran because she's a fool. Foolish emotion. She had little to gain and everything to

41

lose. She would have led the family business. All you need to know is that I am either your worst nightmare, or your best guide. No more meeting behind my back." Then she said to a guard, "Get her out of here."

With that, the meeting was over.

I knew Anne had betrayed me. She called when I went to my room. I answered the phone to keep up appearances. *When the right time comes, I'll drive my vengeance deep.*

8. ALONE IN THE WOODS

The next morning, wishing to be alone, I took to the woods after breakfast. I didn't know what to feel. I sipped my coffee, walking my favorite path, and kicking leaves as I went. Halfway through the woods, I spied a cell phone hidden in the hollow of a tree stump. My heart missed a beat. It had a pink case.

It's Rachel's!

Gazing around, I spotted no one.

Was this a trick? This is where I regularly walk. Could Rachel have known I often walk this path alone?

The message on the screen read, "I haven't given up hope, Alexia. Let's consider this round two. Now we have to be more careful."

I looked to set it on vibrate, but it was already set to that. I went to turn off miscellaneous wireless settings, but they were all already off.

I texted, "I will call you," knowing I couldn't call her yet.

Thank you, God. The fight to free myself from my mother wasn't over. Part of me had given up, but now I don't have to quit. *There is a new fight.*

I walked back with my cup empty of coffee and felt more hopeful, happy even. I might still get my baby sister, Cordelia, out of this.

9. WHAT FELIX SAID

My head was a beehive of worry that night. Restless thoughts buzzed about my mother's wrath, my impending life as a vampire, and a phone from my sister left in the woods… a single sliver of hope.

Then, another bomb dropped on me. Normal, for my life, was out to sea—permanently.

The bomb fell the following day between classes. Anne picked me up for school that morning. She and I were playing the friends game now. I played civil. She still acted like nothing happened.

I sat in the backseat of Anne's car. She frowned into the rear view mirror. "Cute, Alexia, I'm not your chauffeur. Your mother will not want you to act out of the norm. Sit in the front."

I didn't move at first. But then, I realized she might report my behavior back to Mother. *I need to pick my battles*. Without a word or eye contact, I sat up front. She drove.

"Now that you know what you really are, your mother wants me to teach you some things," she said, driving past the gates of my mother's property. "I'm not the only vampire at our school. Meet me in the advanced history classroom after school." She didn't follow-up with who she meant. I didn't want to talk, but I wondered.

Anne and I didn't share the first class, so we split up. I was glad for that. I hoped to be the old me again and not worry about turning and possibly hurting someone.

But after first period, I got a text on my personal phone, not my sister's. I left that in the corner of my walk-in closet. I didn't recognize the number.

Unknown Number: Rachel is your sister.

My heart jumped. Who was this, I wondered. I texted back, mindful to be careful of my words.

Me: Who is this?

Unknown Number: Felix.

I scanned the busy hallway. Felix looked at me from outside his class, standing by a row of lockers. *No, no, no. I can't get him in trouble, too.* I glanced up and down the hallway for Anne or anyone else who might be watching. Anne had said that another vampire attended the school. I wished I'd asked her who.

No one appeared to be noticing us. I strolled up

to Felix and took him by the arm to an empty chemistry lab. People definitely noticed me taking Felix into the classroom, but something about Felix getting involved made me snap.

I made him sit. I stood.

First, I wanted to know how he heard that Rachel was my sister. Next, how much did he know? "Felix, where did you hear that?"

"I heard a rumor that you thought she was your sister. Someone overheard you talking with your boyfriend during the party, and so I followed up. I looked at your picture of her online. It's a match."

"Well, she's not. My real sister is fifteen years older than me."

"Then why did drag me here if it's just a lie. You'd just think I was stupid otherwise."

Good point. I need to keep my emotions in check. "Felix, look—"

Felix thrust out his hands. "Please, don't lie to me. You know too, don't you?"

I poked my head out the doorway and looked up and down the hall for Anne. She wasn't in sight. *I can't throw away an ally. I have almost none, and I have many enemies, some I don't even know yet. No one will suspect him.* "Fine, what do you *think* you know?"

"Both our parents are vampires," Felix said.

Oh gosh, he does know. How long has he known? And how? I'm pretty smart. I should have known sooner than him. He's a freshman. "I'm not saying you're right, but how do you know this?"

His gaze dropped to his shoes, "I saw something...bad."

When he didn't add anything to that, I crossed my arms and said, "Say it."

"I was sneaking around the house where I wasn't supposed to be. I found a freezer. Someone was in it, dead. That's when I knew I didn't really know my parents."

Oh, my. That's a big secret. "I'm so sorry, Felix. But that doesn't mean our parents are vampires."

"No, it doesn't. I bugged the hallway leading to the office in my house. I didn't get much at first. But, after listening for hours, I discovered our parents are something strange. I wasn't sure until somebody said the "v" word. Did you know both our families have power over much of the Northwest?"

Whoa. No, I didn't.

We said nothing for a second. I liked Felix. Having him know made me feel less alone. Yes, Rachel knew, but she's not part of my *normal* life.

"So our parents are vampires," Felix said. "I've wondered if either of you would find out for about two years." His shoulders sank. "It's been hard being the only one to know. I always thought your sister, Cordelia, would find out first, being that she's always the one getting in trouble."

"Hey, I get in trouble, too," I said, sitting down.

"Not like she does."

Got that right.

"Why didn't you tell your brother?"

He shook his head. "He wouldn't take it well."

The bell rang. Tardy. *But who cares about class?*

"Tell no one," I said.

"I've kept the secret for years. I can keep it a little longer."

That's true. I've just found someone that may turn out to be a great ally.

I had to ask. "Are you…" I couldn't quite finish the question.

"A vampire?" he asked finishing my question.

"Yeah, are you?" I asked.

"No."

Good.

10. AFTER SCHOOL SPECIAL

I was nervous about meeting this new vampire. Anne mentioned that another vampire attended school and that I'd meet her. Part of me wished I had told Felix about the meeting. Having someone know what I was going to do would be smart. While I walked the crowded school halls, it hit me that the vampire might be one of five people in Cordelia's inner circle of friends.

There was one person I considered most likely, the smartest one in her circle of friends, May. She often talked my sister out of getting into trouble. She used the term "swell" once and mentioned that she liked *I Love Lucy*. *That means she's old.*

I opened the door to my advanced history class.

Sure enough, May was standing over a desk. My friend Anne sat next to her.

Anne waved me in, "Quick, close and lock the

door."

May looked up from her tablet. "Hey, Alexia. I've been waiting for you to find out about everything."

On the tablet, I saw pictures of students.

"Anne tells me you are about to turn," May said.

I nodded. I knew her, but just met her then as a vampire. How often does she kill people? Can she be trusted? Anne seemed to think so, but I don't really know Anne. This might get scary.

"Well, um, Anne said you needed to learn about the vampire world," she said.

"Yes," I said. My silence may have made her uncomfortable.

"Okay, I'm what you call a scout. I find people that would fit well into Houses. Or join covens of rich vampires. I worked with your mother, in fact. I got your head body guard right out of high school."

Anne knocked her foot against May's leg. Anne frowned as if she wasn't supposed to mention the bodyguard. *What's that about?*

She continued, "Well, I've been going to high school for 20 years now. And I've been responsible for recruiting many movers and shakers."

"Wow. That must be fun." I hated myself the second I said it.

She frowned a bit. "Yes, it can be."

"How do you know someone should become a vampire?" I asked.

"We look for charm, beauty, strong will, desire to impress, intelligence, and also loyal team players."

I am not loyal to my mother. I am a team player only when I see fit. And I have never shown a strong desire to impress others.

"So, did my mother put you up to befriending my sister?"

She smiled and said, "Yes, but it's been easy for me. I love your sister... she's like a little sibling to me."

I saw that she really meant it. How could she not?

Was that a real answer? She had spent two decades at high schools. That makes her an infiltrator. She plays a part for people who have unsavory intent.

"Thanks, it's been interesting," I said.

But I didn't really mean it. It was only scratching the surface. *How often has she killed someone the day before and come to school like nothing's wrong? I didn't know.*

"Let's take you home," Anne said with a smile. Another reminder that I am a prisoner to a fate I am only beginning to understand.

None of this felt right. *For Cordelia's sake, I will run. And take Felix with me.*

11. ANNE'S HOUSE

This is stupid. I'm about to break into my best friend's house. Scratch that—former best friend's house. I think it's Anne's anyway. She never let me visit, insisting she felt embarrassed by her "drunken wretch of a mother." She likely lied to help form a common bond with me over how I loathed my bitter mother. I suspect she lives alone.

I've got good reasons for breaking in. If I'm to escape my mother's grasp, I need to know who Anne really is. She was hired to watch me and pretend to be my friend. She separated me from Rachel. She appeared to be 17, but what is her true age? The older she is, the harder it will be to outsmart her. This was risky, but doing nothing drove me crazy.

An online search told me the owner of this house had Anne's last name. Maybe she bought it under a different name. It was thirty minutes away from home, and she once said it was a 30-minute drive to my place. The home's exterior appeared nice in a comfortably middle class sort of way. The simple home had one floor and a well-kept yard. Its trees blocked any view of neighbors.

If this was Anne's house, she shouldn't be home for another 45 minutes. Anne secretly meets with my mom on Fridays. *For an hour! Even I don't think I'm that interesting, and I'm a teenager.*

I told Mother I'd be at a friend's house. So, I had an alibi for being out late.

I plucked up the courage to knock. I needed to, just in case this proved to be someone else's house.

Silence.

No one is home. At least no one is answering. Okay, this is where it gets real. I felt numb turning the knob. *That's it, I'm a criminal!* I found the door unlocked. *That's weird. Everyone locks their doors. But Anne's a vampire, and therefore a predator. Maybe she doesn't fear break-ins.* I'd planned on busting a door or window and making it look like a robbery. Now, I didn't need to. I stepped into a living room, careful to keep my gloves on. I didn't want to leave fingerprints behind.

If this is Anne's house, I don't know her. It looked old, like my mother's side of the mansion. No computer or television. A lone antique cream-colored loveseat centered the room. Woodcarvings framed the top of the seat. The wooden legs were crafted to look like a beast's paws. *It's expensive, elegant, but not modern.* The loveseat faced three bookshelves. With a single seat in the living room, it felt lonely.

I scanned the living room for evidence I'd discovered Anne's house and not a stranger's with a retro sense of decor. On the wall, I spotted a picture of Anne. She wore a dress I bought for her. I bought it for her birthday, which meant the picture was recent. Her friend in the picture shared Anne's light complexion, a fellow vampire, perhaps?

My heart thumped hard. Behind my former best friend's back, I'm getting to know the real Anne. I took a bit of cruel pleasure in doing this small act of revenge. She pretended to be a friend, and I opened up to her. Now, I'm getting the truth of who she *really* is.

Mystery novels filled several shelves. I spotted romance books, as well, lots of 'em. I hated that genre. She must have hid her love of romance, knowing my disdain. *Sappy predictable junk.* Almost all were paperbacks. *I loathe old paperbacks with their wrinkled spines, they're depressing.*

I spotted several books we'd read by our favorite author, *Chelsea and Swindle, Children of Nod,* she had a busted copy of a book in the same universe as *Children of Nod,* I forget the title. *Nikki of Camden, The God Conspiracy,* and the last book I got her, *Memoirs of a Missing Year.*

Several shelves of vinyl records stood along another wall. One album I'd bought for her at the mall.

Like her paperback books and records, her collection spanned several decades. I tried to judge her age by what she owned. Since the records spanned the 20th century, my guess was she's very old. *That's decades of experience I don't have. I must seem stupid to her.*

Wanting to be quick, I dashed down the hall looking for her bedroom. Halfway, I stopped to look into what appeared to be a guest bedroom. With its door ajar, it didn't look used. *I'm lucky she doesn't have anyone living with her.*

At the end of the hall, I discovered the master bedroom. Clothes were in the open closet. *This is Anne's room.*

I searched for a photo album. I figured vampires don't have paperwork like birth certificates. *How far back the photos go can tell me how old she is.* At the bottom of a dresser, I discovered a leather-bound photo album. In it were dozens of black and white pictures of Anne, the oldest faded out to brown. She stood by a car. Its body resembled a horse pulled carriage, rather than a modern car. The carriage had no cover and the wheels had spokes. Her outfit was elegant and yet very old-timey. *The era must be 1910s, maybe. She lived in a city. Where? I didn't know. Was she still human in these photos?*

So I know she's old. She must hate acting like a kid. I must seem like a child to her while inside, she has the perspective of a great, great, great grandmother.

Do vampires age mentally?

Anne's meeting with my mother will be ending. I needed to leave soon.

I walked by a record player. I hadn't noticed it when I left the living room. It stood on four legs and was about four feet tall. It wasn't plugged into the wall, but had a hand crank instead. The hand crank must power it. She must like the music of her era and keeps this old player so she can listen to it.

Anger gripped me for a second as I considered breaking the record. The record read *Flamenco* by Frankie Lane. *Never heard of it. This is one of her few connections with the past and if I take it, she might not be able to find another. Can I do that? I don't want to be so cruel.*

I left, being careful not to leave a trace that I'd been there.

12. THE CURSE OF THE BITE

Anne stared at me from across the school lunch table. We sat alone. I kept my gaze on my food. I'd known her long enough to know she was mad. Seldom did I see her vexed.

"Alexia, did you know that vampires have a great sense of smell?" Anne glared.

"Should I be taking notes?" I asked.

"I smelled an intruder in my house last night. She must have known I was gone, meeting with your mother."

I shrugged and tried not to look scared. This could get back to Mother, if it hadn't already.

"I smell your increased perspiration," Anne scowled.

I fixed my gaze on her and tried to look brave.

"Why did you do it? Why did you break into my home?" Anne asked.

"I wanted to know who had pretended to be my friend since middle school."

Her gaze turned soft. The cheek muscles relaxed. She looked sad, her eyes narrowing. "Your mother hired me to keep an eye on you and be your friend, but I actually do *like* you."

"But you're decades older than me."

"Haven't you liked people younger than yourself? Yes, I have many years of experience and understanding, but I'm still mentally a teenager. That's 'The Curse of the Bite;' my brain is forever wired like a teenager's." After I didn't say anything, she continued, "Please, don't invade my home again. It's the one place I have that's all mine."

For the first time in a while, I knew Anne not as a conspirator or a vampire, but just as Anne. "I won't."

She tilted her head. "I won't tell your mother, but you can't be reckless. Each of your sisters might be your mother's right hand. Rachel ran away. You are her second choice and still could be her *final* choice. But your sister, Cordelia, can replace you in that role. I am your best ally at work in your House of Bathory."

Anne wanted that to motivate me, instead it scared me. *I'm damaged goods in my mother's eyes. She's likely eying Cordelia already. I couldn't let that happen. To see my mother shred away Cordelia's innocence would be terrible. Mother's left her marks on me. I hurt nice boys, like Jonathan, and love the wrong ones. I'm also ill-tempered.*

But there is hope in Cordelia, a girl who likes to draw, who still watches cartoons, she might still be saved.

I looked across the table. How much fear did Anne see? Did she know my thoughts were of Cordelia, or did she think I was just worried for myself?

"Tell me what I need to know to get back on my mother's good side." I have to know the rules of the vampire world.

"Okay." Anne said. She briefed me on some of the rules. "First, keep the fact that vampires exist a secret."

Obvious. That goes without saying.

"Vampires pay tribute to the Houses that rule over them," Anne said. "There's something of a hierarchy. Royals, like you and the Ruthven', on top."

Yay. Felix is royal too. I gotta tell him.

Anne continued, "Then, traditionally, people working close to the royals. Next, the rich business class, though with recent centuries, their standing has improved. Rich business leaders in the vampire community have rivaled the riches of minor houses, but royals still looked down on them nonetheless. Next, there's the working class and last, nomads. North America has a lot of what are called American Nomads. There are a number of vampire legends about them."

Later, after school, I met with Felix. We tricked his older brother, Lionel, into arranging it. I had Felix ask Lionel if I could help him with math. Math would be our cover. Lionel agreed to ask, and to his surprise, I said, "Yes."

We studied in Felix's room.

"I swept for bugs." Felix said.

"You think your parents will spy on you?" *It says a lot about my life that it's not the weirdest thing I've heard.*

"Yeah. They drink blood, so thinking the worst seems... prudent."

Good point.

His room was really neat. I suspect he cleaned it knowing I'd visit. The room smelled aired out. I wondered if he made it neat because he wanted to make a good impression, being a teenage boy and all.

"Look, you need to stay away from Anne." I said. "She's a vampire. There is one other in the school, it's May Winters."

"Whoa, I was thinking of asking her to a dance!"

"Well, she won't hurt you, you're a royal."

"Then maybe I should. Being nice to a royal is in her best interest." He looked quite amused with himself.

I felt anger flare up. *He's not taking this seriously.*

"Yes, I should ask her. If she says yes, my profile will be higher with other girls."

Oh, gosh. Do all boys think like this? Felix is thinking of this like a social chess match for status and opportunity. He's schemed out a post-prom dating situation, and he hasn't even asked the girl out yet.

"Kidding," he said.

"No, you're not. You're a guy," I said, crossing my arms.

"Or maybe your sister. That makes sense, we'll be a power couple from two great Houses. Maybe our parents will arrange it in order to keep peace with two royal Houses."

"Felix, I'll turn into a vampire before you do, you remember that, right? I'm biting you first, that's a promise."

He smiled. "I'll take my chances. Hey, what is May doing in school?"

"She's a scout to find good potential vampires to turn."

"Whoa."

"Yeah. What's with the green military boxes?" The boxes were peeking out from under his bed.

"They're ammo boxes, so, yeah, umm… before I knew you knew—"

"Which was yesterday," I said with a smirk.

"Okay, long before I knew you knew, like a year ago, I looked into survival stuff... just in case I needed to run away."

"You were gonna run off with weapons?"

"Yeah."

"That's a bad idea."

"On my own, yes, but if I do, maybe you'll come with me," Felix said.

If Rachel doesn't come, maybe I'll have to run away. No, that's stupid. Things might turn for the worse. Mother will kill me. I'd never see Cordelia again.

"Show me what you have, if that's okay. And may I borrow some of your stuff?"

I looked at his bookshelf; much of it was standard geek fare, but some books were not very Felix-ish, a self-defense book on Krav Maga, vanishing without-a-trace books, and survival books. I knew Felix. These books didn't reflect his personality; instead, they reflected his worries. He must have spent long nights fretting about the true identity of his parents. *Did he fear his parents? Did he worry they might kill him? Or was his fear of who he might hurt if he turned?* Then, I realized how lucky I was. I had my sister, Rachel, just long enough to get some perspective. Felix knew just enough truth to scare him, and he'd known the truth alone.

He must have wanted to run away, but never had the courage to do it. *Yet, will I? If I do, I'll take him along. I owe him, and he deserves better.*

"Maybe let me borrow a survival book, and one of those "how to disappear" books."

I decided. I'm running, and not waiting for Mother's next move!

13. DRAWINGS BY MY SISTER

I didn't know how to feel about Anne. That night, she hung out at my house. Her company saved me from being alone and worrying about being a vampire someday soon.

While Anne and I streamed some television, Cordelia came into the living room.

"Alexia, I've been meaning to give this to you," Cordelia said. She showed me a picture she'd drawn.

Her skill was beyond her years. Even Mother praised her talent. But, this one made my heart stop. She had drawn me, Rachel, and Anne, at the restaurant. The picture showed the moment that Rachel texted me a message.

This made no sense, Cordelia wasn't there at the meeting, how did she draw this? Weirder, the picture date was two weeks before the events took place.

"Wow, I love it, thanks." I put all my courage into those words so as not to sound nervous.

Cordelia left with a smile.

I set the picture on the coffee table.

"So what did your sister send you?" Anne asked.

"A picture, you saw it," I said.

"No. I was talking about the text. Your mother has known about Cordelia's ability to draw things she hasn't seen. She drew your meeting with Rachel a week before she showed up."

I paused the show. "It was a simple message... Don't give up."

"Really?"

"Anne, you were there, do you think she had time to draw out blueprints to an elaborate plan against the House of Bathory?"

Anne nodded, "No, you're right."

I hope that proved to be the end of it.

Anne sat up. "Let's go see what else she drew."

"Mom's already checked, I'm sure."

Anne shrugged. "Cordelia's ability is sporadic, if you can call it an ability. Your mom has seldom found her drawings useful. In fact, the one of you and Rachel is the only one that proved useful. It helped me find you at the restaurant."

That explains how she found me.

We went to my sister's room. This made me nervous. What if Cordelia drew pictures of me running away?

We knocked on Cordelia's door.

Silence, then, "Come in."

She sat playing a video game, her headset on.

I asked if we might look at her pictures. She nodded, wearing a headset, so she didn't want to talk and confuse her teammates online.

Anne took a stack of a dozen drawings from her desk. The first one showed me at a bank vault with the key I'd found in the old book of *Peter and Wendy. Bank vaults don't take old-timey keys.* Cordelia had dated this picture today.

The next one showed me in the country. My back turned while I faced a two-story house. I knew it was me because the clothes and shoes were mine. In my hand was what looked like a map.

At the sight of the next picture, the color ran from my face. If her drawings proved to be correct, things get worse.

Anne's expression looked worried too. "Crazy.

Maybe there's nothing to the drawings after all."

Anne started to set the pictures down, but I took them. *No, maybe there is something to them. But what?*

14. BLOODY FOOTPRINTS IN SNOW

Cordelia's last drawing possessed the most detail I'd seen in any of her works. As soon as Anne left, I went back and looked in on my sister, still playing her video game. I thought she'd been able to remain innocent despite Mother's verbal abuse, but no one could draw this and be innocent inside.

It reminded me of medieval paintings of hell. In it, a single girl walked barefoot in the snow, leaving bloody footprints behind. The girl looked over her shoulder with fear on her face. Grey fog consumed any view of the distant background.

Next to the girl, in a house with torn walls, a man sat in a chair, his lower half-frozen and his upper torso in flames. Even underneath the ice, fire raged. A woman in the house stood with a knife in her hand. The blade dripped blood. Two small children looked up to her, their lips sliced open from the corners to show smiles. Though the woman's head was turned slightly, two flames licked from her eyes like fire bursting from windows.

I returned my attention to the girl. Oddly, her feet were not bloody, despite the trail she left. I remembered overhearing one of my teachers talk about a drawing a kid made in my class. They were disturbing, too. She thought they meant something bad about my fellow student's state of mind. I wondered if the girl must represent Cordelia, even if she doesn't mean it to. Therefore, the chaos *in the picture is her rage and sadness.*

In the background, two shadows walk on the side of the road. Even as shadows, their bodies were contorted.

I didn't want this, but I needed to talk to Cordelia. *She's going through the same thing I am with Mother. I allowed myself to believe she was okay, but now I needed to talk with her. She's in pain.*

"Cordelia, stop the game. We need to talk."

She faced my direction, her headset still on. "Gotta go, guys." Then she answered someone online, "Oh, whatever." She took off her headset. "What's up, Alexia?"

I showed her the drawing. "Tell me about this picture."

Her eyes widened. "Nothing, I just drew it."

She's being evasive, I'll have to be easy on her if I am going to be able to get her to talk about her feelings without upsetting her. I sat down. "Tell me how you felt drawing this."

She turned her gaze away.

"It's okay," I said.

"Mom asks me about my pictures. She seems to think I know things I don't."

"Did she ask about this one?"

"No, she seemed to think it was just a drawing."

Count on Mother to overlook her child's pain when she's too busy trying to see the future. "But it's not just a drawing to you?"

"Don't tell Mom."

"I won't."

"I don't remember drawing it. My first memory of it is with me sitting at my desk. Ink still drying on my hands."

She must be burying her pain, using her art as an outlet. I didn't know what to say.

"He was trying to save her," Cordelia continued.

"Who?"

"I don't know his name, but he's not bad. He once looked for the bloody footprint girl. I don't know how I know, but this picture is his memory, whoever he is."

"This picture isn't real, Cordelia."

"I don't know what it is." Cordelia stood and took a picture from her dresser. The picture showed the same house Cordelia drew before. I'd been standing in front in the other picture. But where I stood, a man took my place. He had brown hair, wore a t-shirt and blue jeans. I saw the house half covered in ice, while flames burst through the windows.

"I think he will find us," Cordelia said.

15. WALKING TERROR

Cordelia's fantasies bothered me; she believed a strange man might find us. Wherever he goes, strange terror follows. Cordelia said this man was good, but her pictures suggest him to be a walking hell.

Mother's wrath had already taken a toll on my sister. We need to go.

I marched to my desk and started writing things down. On a piece of paper, I made two columns. Reasons to run and not to run.

Run: Cordelia sees the future. She can reveal our actions beforehand. So, I need to run soon.

Not to Run: I am clueless about being a vampire.

And related to that...

Not to Run: I have not even turned yet.

Run: Waiting will make it less likely.

Not the best reason.

Not to run:

I can't think of anything. I trust no one in my family but Cordelia. My best friend is hired to watch me.

Run: Mother is evil.

Run: She's a killer, and if you stay, she might make you one.

With the picture Cordelia drew showing her state of mind and looking at my pros and cons, I decided. *We run in three days.*

I had to get Anne off my back, if that were possible. I went to bed with the gears turning. I knew I might not sleep that night, but I knew I'd not give up the fight for me, my sister, and Felix.

16. FOLLOWING THE PICTURES

Lying in bed and doing nothing didn't make me happy. On the other hand, I wanted time to think. Time grew short for me, and the picture Cordelia drew showed that Mom's tyranny was taking a toll on my younger sister. Also... I might turn soon.

Time... when I turn I'll have lots of that. Anne is like a hundred or something and looks like she can model for H&M.

I looked at my clock; it no longer ticks. It's an old antique, and I rarely bothered to use the keys to wind it. Antique clocks needed special keys to wind them up.

Keys! Rachel left a key that looks like a clock key. I snatched the old clock from the table, but the key didn't fit. *Of course not, this is my clock, not Rachel's.*

Maybe, the keys are for her clock, which is in Rachel's old room. After Rachel left years ago, her room remained all but abandoned. Only Anne slept in it occasionally.

If the key is for a hidden compartment, it won't be the front face of the clock.

I turned it around. I found a keyhole on the back. All antique clocks had a big back door, for some reason. The key turned with little resistance. The door opened, inside lay a folded piece of paper, and a safe deposit key. *This must have waited for thirteen years to be found!*

Dear Alexia and Cordelia,

I hope you both find this. Know I left without wanting to. Take the key and go to the address below. Go to vault 132, and in that vault you will find your means to freedom. Keep the clock key, you'll still need it.

I drove to the bank. Once the safe deposit box was opened, I peered inside. On top, a pistol with a silencer. Beneath that, a note lay on top of cash: a lot of cash. *There must be thousands of dollars here.*

Alexia and Cordelia,

If you read this, chances are I'm dead.

Dead? I hope not. I just guessed about what the key was for.

There is a deed to a house under the cash.

At first, I tried to gather the cash in my arms, cradling it like a little baby. My only hope was that no one saw me with $15,000 in my arms. I peeked my head out the vault door and requested a bag. Then, with a bag of cash and a deed to a house in hand, I marched out, victorious.

The drive to the house listed on the deed took several hours. I passed a town called Morton. On the way, I missed two calls from Mother.

I turned on a gravel road and parked.

I exited the car and looked at the two-story house. The clothes I wore and the house matched the picture Cordelia drew. But I didn't hold a map in my hand like I'd guessed when I first saw the picture; instead, I held the deed. *So far Cordelia's drawings are correct.*

One question bothered me. *Does this mean that the strange man Cordelia drew will follow?*

17. A LITTLE PIECE OF FREEDOM

Things were sparse inside the house. No TV, an unplugged fridge, a couch in both the den and the living room. The smell of dust hung everywhere. It was perfect.

Upstairs, I found five bedrooms. *One bathroom on the second floor, meaning I'd need to share, terrible. I'd take the big room at the end of the hall. Don't judge. I have no idea how middle class teens have everything in such a small space…. And I don't want to learn.*

Mother called. "Where are you?"

"Look, I need time alone. Being a half-vampire is a lot to swallow. I'm just taking time to think things through."

"Very well, child. You should know we will likely capture Rachel. We suspect she is tied to another House."

"Don't harm her."

"What?"

I had to think up a reason my mother might accept. "She is tied to another House. She will be valuable to both. Her bond of blood to us and loyalty to them can work in our favor."

"You may yet make a good right hand, Alexia. See you Sunday night."

That last part told me I'd only have a day to get things ready.

What good is running away if you don't have the power to protect that choice? Time to buy guns.

I drove to a strange store. Think of a Saks 5th Avenue for rednecks. Thanks to the ancient Egyptian miracle called taxidermy, dead animals decorated this hunting, fishing, and "shoot-the-burglar-in-the-face-store."

Guns were on the second floor. I bought a sniper rifle for my sister and AR-15s for the rest of us. Also, all of us got shotguns and Glocks for close combat. All weapons bought in cash. Knowing what guns to buy and to pay in cash proved that reading Felix's survival books and those long nights thinking of the worst had paid off.

I didn't want my sister to see direct action, hence the sniper rifle. However, she'd have to fight. Both families seemed able to summon a small army with the money they had.

After making a stop for some food, I dropped off the guns and ammo at the empty house. *Home. My small piece of freedom. Thank you, Rachel.*

Later that night, I looked at the moon rising above the trees that stood about four stories tall. Alone in the empty house, I turned the seat in the living room toward the windows while looking at the stars in the dark. I ate chicken I'd cooked myself, a skill that might prove useless soon. As a vampire, I'd have little need to eat.

I wondered if there might be truth to Cordelia's last picture with the strange man standing outside this home. If so, when would he come?

I texted Cordelia to see how she was doing. Then Rachel called me from her phone.

"Hello."

"Where are you?" Rachel said. I heard nervousness in her voice.

"At the house you left for me."

"You found that? I'm cornered. Mom's going to take me in. I'm in Bellevue."

I heard a thud on the other end.

"I'm hours away."

"Look. I may not have long. Don't think like a teenager; think like a vampire."

"Okay."

"They aren't going to kill me right away. I need

you go to my apartment on 12th Street in Bellevue and pick up a gun."

"You left one in the bank vault. It has a silencer."

"I need you to get me out. Use the lost phone app on your phone. It will find me."

"I can't shoot people." *What am I saying? I just bought an arsenal of guns.*

Another hard last thud followed by men yelling on the other end.

Rachel screamed.

Click.

I looked around the house, *my* empty house.

I'm going to kill Mom.

18. BITE ME!

I panicked. *I've no idea what to do. Rachel needs me. Mother's minions have her.*

But will I be quick enough?

What if she's already dead?

The phone Rachel had given me rang.

"Rachel, what happened?" I screamed.

"Hello Alexia." A woman's voice spoke. She sounded calm, with a side of smug. "Fiona gives you two choices…."

Bullshit. Mom only gives me one choice: "Do as I want or screw you." That's just one.

The woman continued "… Run and never return, and lose the family name. Or come to the address I'll text you. Kill Rachel and prove your loyalty. You will be your

Mother's right hand. Please know that I am to turn you as well. Your mother believes your time as a human is over."

I almost fell back. I closed my eyes.

This is my life. I will be a human as long as I damn well please!

A text gave me directions. I set my phone's map app to give me directions to that location.

You've just made your own noose, lady! I've one advantage. Everyone thinks I won't shoot them.

I needed to slow down twice, finding myself driving 85 mph. *That's not legal anywhere.* No one stopped me, thankfully.

Once there, I tucked the gun into the back of my jeans. The cool metal clung to the small of my back. Finally, I put my leather jacket on top.

It's on the second story of a building that looks like cheap office spaces. I climb the metal stairs. At the door, I knock.

I wait.

Silence.

I open the door.

"Good, Alexia," said the now familiar female voice from the phone call. She stood about six-foot and appeared thirty something. Dirty blonde hair hung just below her shoulders. A dead-serious faced reminds me of one of my teachers who was never happy. "Come in. This is not a trap. You have a choice—"

I whipped out my Glock.

Her eyes widen and her body stiffened as her eyes fixed on my gun.

Shoot the leg? Hard target. Center mass? I don't want to be a killer. Make it the leg.

Shzzt. The silencer stifles the shot to a sneeze.

To my shock, blood reddened her leg. I hit! Thank God silencers are legal in Washington.

She falls.

She'll live.

I walked in. "Where is my sister?"

She cursed at me. I point my gun to her other thigh.

"Around the corner," she said.

Nothing like threats of physical violence to gain respect.

Before I passed her, she grabbed my leg. Then pulled up my pant leg and bit her thin front teeth into my ankle.

I yelped and fired.

A mask of blood covered her face. The bullet hit her head. Her eyes empty of life.

I killed her. I did it. Why didn't I aim elsewhere? If I'd thought and not reacted, maybe she might be hurt, but still living. I'm a killer. What's wrong with me?

Blood drips down my ankle where her blood mixed with the bite. I ignore the pain and limped on. I found Rachel tied to the chair in an empty room. I pulled off her gag.

"Thanks. She was going to turn you," Rachel said.

"She bit me," I said, while I untied her.

"You let her bite you? Damn it," Rachel said.

"What?" I knew even as I asked.

"You mean you don't feel it?"

I did. My ankle felt like fire ants had bitten me. A wildfire inched up my leg.

When I undid the last knot, the fire reached the middle of my body. "Rachel, I might need you to carry me out."

Then the burn reached my heart. The fire turned to ice. I felt cold, very cold. Each beat of my heart gushed chilly liquid.

Then, everything went black.

19. JUICE BOXES, LOTS OF 'EM

I recall being cold while I remained unconscious. My whole being lay smothered in a chill that even bit at my marrow.

Slowly, a warmth invaded the cold, starting in my chest, reaching out to my limbs. The fog of my mind faded, lifting away the haze.

Where am I? Why am I so thirsty?

"Wake up," a voice called me.

Who is that?

Why am I lying on carpet? The carpet felt rough and hurt my cheek.

I heard a strange sound, like mechanical sneezes. Followed by thuds. Groans. Two more of the mechanical sounds are followed by silence. My foggy mind allowed me to remember that my silencer made that sound.

"We need to move, Alexia. I don't know if they called for reinforcements." I realized that it's Rachel's voice.

She pulled me to my feet. My eyes opened and I saw two people lying dead. One, I knew worked in Mother's wing of the house. I passed the woman I killed. She had bitten me. *I'm a killer, and that knowledge isn't going away. Worse, I'm not sure I should feel bad.*

Rachel pulled me to the door.

I wanted to ask what's going on, but I knew it wasn't the time. She seemed worried.

"Do you think you can make it to the car?" Rachel asked.

"Yeah," I managed.

I slept most of the drive.

My sister Rachel took me to a safe house, a motel in Seattle. I barely remember the trip. I don't recall her carrying me into the room. Those first few days, I'd felt pangs of thirst, and it felt like thousands of needles filled my muscles, causing me to hurt. Fortunately, I slept through much of it. Rachel sated my thirst with blood bags. After drinking, I slept. Rest took me away from the constant pain. That lasted two days.

Out the window of my motel room, I gazed at a cloudless Seattle day. My view of the city consisted of rundown buildings. People don't think of this part of town when they envision the city.

The pain eased, and my need for blood *had* subsided. Yet, the need to feed, while lessened, still tore at my self-control. So, Rachel didn't let me leave her sight. As far as I was concerned, all the people outside were walking juice boxes. I had to keep telling myself, *I'm not a monster, this is just the thirst talking.* But the thirst spoke really loud!

"Don't even think about it, Alexia," Rachel said, trying to pass the time with television.

"Oh, I am."

"Here, have one early." She trotted to the fridge and got a blood bag. She'd been feeding me every hour using an egg timer.

I hated the timer, tic, tic, tic, tic…. Why couldn't she use the phone app? "I wonder what pimp blood tastes like?"

"Not funny," Rachel said.

I thought it was.

"Here, sis." Rachel offered a blood bag.

I didn't move from the window, fixated on a sleazy guy with a cigarette behind his ear. *I wonder if smokers' blood tastes different?*

"Over here Alexia, you're not sucking on a blood bag near the window."

Oh, if the people walking by saw me.

I snatched the blood bag, and while I drained it, the urge to feed melted away and a feeling of normalcy returned to me. Dopamine flooded my system, too. Rachel said that's what *can* make killing addictive.

"Do all vampires use donated blood?" I asked.

"Many do. Why do you think the Red Cross is always short on blood?"

Oh, that does make sense.

With my head cleansed of most of the urge to feed, my mind turned to important matters. "When do we make our next move against Mother?" I asked.

"I don't know. She's going to be on full alert now. She'll be watching Cordelia," Rachel said.

Killing hired henchmen tends to put your enemies on full alert. "Let's give Felix a burner phone to give to Cordelia."

We planned it out. I texted Felix and told him we were hiding a phone for him at the public library. He needed to give it to Cordelia.

Felix texted right back.

Felix: A dead drop!

Me: ?

Felix: In spycraft, it's a method of passing things to agents.

Nerds, and their endless weird vocabulary.

Felix: Something has happened hasn't it? You

can't just meet her can you? Does she know about vampires yet?

Me: No.

Felix: What happened? You didn't come to school?

Alexia: I got turned.

Felix: How?

A jumble of words burst forth from the dam of my mind. *What do I tell? How do I tell? Mother kidnapped my sister, Rachel, so I needed to kill someone to free her. I killed the person who turned me, and that happened two days ago.*

I haven't processed all that yet.

How horrible is that? Someone who had a big part in changing the direction of my life is dead. I didn't know her. I didn't hate her, but she's dead. Should I hate her?

I still had to text back an answer.

Me: I wish I could tell you, but it's so big I feel the need to tell you in person.

Felix: I'll get it to her.

Me: Thanks.

Rachel left the phone in a book by gutting the pages. The phone fit snug so it wouldn't move around inside or fall out if opened. She didn't actually destroy a library book, but rather we brought a book to the library and put it on the shelf. How did we know it wasn't going to be taken before Felix got it? We didn't, but how often are 99% of the books touched at a library? Really, think about that one. It was a pretty safe bet.

That evening, I paced in the motel room. I didn't want to talk to Rachel. My wish was to straighten out the knots in my head. *How do you tell Cordelia that the impossible has happened? That you aren't fully human, if that?*

Instead of figuring that out, Rachel's tablet played a jingle signaling Cordelia's burner calling. I opened video chat. Cordelia looked shocked. She slapped her hand on her mouth. She must have noticed my pale skin. Does she know?

"Cordelia, I've something to tell you I—"

"Mom did it. She turned you," Cordelia said.

"How did you..." stupid question. Mother must have started teaching her the truth. "No, it wasn't Mom. She hired someone. What you need to know is things are going to be okay. But we need to get away from Mom. I have a place we can go."

"Where?"

"A place we can be safe. I can't tell you yet. Are you ready? Will you come with me?"

"Alexia, I hate Mom more than you do."

That's a yes.

I recognized the background. She was in a study room at school. *Great. A place she can be alone. Smart choice.*

With that out of the way, I needed to lay out the plan of their escape. I told Cordelia that Felix would be joining us. I opened chat with Felix.

"Okay," Felix said, "she knows everything?"

"Whoa," Cordelia said, "how long have you known?"

"Too long," Felix said, with no pride in his voice, but a hint of weariness.

Rachel sat beside me so Cordelia could see her. "Hi, sis," she said to Cordelia. She waved back. "Hello Felix." Felix waved. "Vampires have a good sense of smell. That's why we're hiding clothes for you near the school. They're in a bag full of leaves. That'll cover your smell. An Uber cars is scheduled to pick you up at the first address. Once it drops you off, another driver will pick you up at the second location to take you to your final stop. On both trips you are to look for people following you."

"What if they are?" Felix asked.

"Contact me. Remember, keep your phones fully charged," Rachel said.

Cordelia's face showed concern. "What are you going to do?"

Rachel looked at me, then back to the two on the screen. "I've got backup."

Cordelia's eyes narrowed. "Another House."

"Yes, one that does not wish to be named. I trust them. I've known them for years. If things go well, we don't need them."

This House must have something to gain by the apparent weakening of the House of Bathory.

"Guys, just go to the address that I've listed below on your screen." Rachel thumped her fist on the table. "Tomorrow you run away."

20. ESCAPE

"You can't be with them, Alexia." Rachel stood and closed the blinds.

"Why not?" I turned away from the window. I knew the reason, but I protested with my question anyway. "I want to see them."

"You know why. The same reason I haven't let you leave this room. You might hurt them."

With a sigh, I asked, "What do I do?"

"You can come, but keep your distance. Do you think you can watch them from a vantage point?"

"Vantage point?"

"Just in case Mother gets her men to ambush us, I'll need you to fire on them. Can you do that?"

I nodded, though I doubted myself. Even with the

blood bags, I'd wanted to bite someone all day. *But thinking of other things might take my mind off the thirst that ate at my will.*

As we drove across town, my urge to bite ebbed enough to feel close to normal.

"What if they get caught? They'll need a cover story," I said.

"I've got that covered." Rachel said. "They will be instructed to leave their secret burner phones on the first ride they get. Then, if they are caught, they'll say they were told to meet with me because I had information about you. Enough of the truth to be believable."

We stopped at our destination, a state park.

Rachel walked around the trees and benches. "This place is secluded. That's good, considering your situation."

With a bag from the trunk slung over her shoulder, she led me into the woods.

"You'll wait here." We were seven yards deep into the forest when Rachel set the bag down and opened it, revealing a sniper rifle.

"But what if someone sees me?"

"No one should." Rachel shoved a sniper rifle and a walkie-talkie at me. "This park doesn't get that many visitors.

So I waited while she stood in the parking lot.

Odd smells drifted in the wind. Something living had brushed against trees and shrubs. Deer, I guessed. Other things smelled of dirt and grass, rabbits perhaps.

Oh, great. Now I've the urge to bite rabbits. Being a vampire sucks!

Taking my mind away from furry food, I scanned the area for Mother's men.

A car crept slowly into the parking lot. It stopped. Careful to keep my finger off the trigger, I looked through the scope, scanning the car's interior, I spotted my sister and, in the shadows, what looked like Felix as he paid the driver. *Good.*

I turned my attention to the edge of the woods. Nothing. I felt useless. Yet someone needed to be watching. When I glanced back, I saw only Cordelia and Felix. Felix's brother, Lionel, didn't come. *Too bad.* The two stood outside the car as it drove away.

Not taking any chances, I returned my attention to the area around them. Still quiet.

"Alexia?" Cordelia spoke on the walkie.

"I'm here. Watching the area. We can't be close yet. I'm newly turned."

"I know."

Of course, I'd just said that when we last talked.

Rachel spoke next. "Cordelia, I want you and

Felix to go to the red car." She said that into the walkie for my benefit. Cordelia and Felix needed to be safe, they needed to go in another car and not be trapped with me.

"I don't have a license," Cordelia shook her head.

"It's okay. It'll drive you," Rachel said. "And here's your license, just in case. But you shouldn't need it."

A car screeched into the parking lot. I readied my rifle. *These are Mom's men. They have to be Mom's men.* I fired into the driver's side of the windshield.

Doors opened on the opposite side of the car. I didn't know where my two sisters and Felix ran. My mind tunneled to my gun and the people around that car.

Shots boomed around me. I thought they might be in the woods, but the echo of gunfire bounced everywhere.

The walkie crackled. "Alexia, one of Mother's men is in the woods. Look out."

I looked around and saw nothing. Just tree branches swaying a bit in the wind. Every little movement caught my attention.

Bam!

A pang rang in my chest. I looked down while blood reddened my shirt. Thirst arose in me with the blood draining. I smelled humans nearby. I scurried away even while pain wracked me.

As I tumbled downhill, darting to the smell, I heard a shriek. Later, someone told me that only I screamed. I turned behind a parked car, seeing two scared faces. I didn't recognize them. The thirst flooded my thinking, so I failed to see my sister and Felix in front of me. I ignored Rachel, who stood in my way, protecting them.

Rachel held me in place. Her lips moved, but I heard nothing.

Another shot thundered.

Black.

21. ALONE IN THE DARK

I awoke to darkness. Only a single sliver of light from twenty feet away provided any illumination. It appeared to be from under a door.

While trying to recall how I got here, I felt two faint aches on my torso.

"You were shot, Alexia, twice." My mother's voice burst from the darkness as if to answer my question. Her tone sounded even and calm, but I felt the anger that brewed underneath her façade.

"Gee, thanks, Mother."

She let out a cold chuckle. "You should thank my men, you were about to kill your sister and Felix. Felix's death might have caused a war with the House of Ruthven."

"What happened to me when I was shot?"

"You turned frenzied, we also call it ravenous. When a vampire's blood level drops too low we no longer think, and go for the quickest source of blood. That is, your sister and the Ruthven boy, Felix."

Thank God no one got hurt. Did Rachel escape?

I felt weak while I tried to stand. My eyes adjusted to the dark. Stuck in my arm, I spotted an IV. I barely felt the needle. The tube led to a blood bag. Looking beyond the blood bag, I spotted bars around me. I'm in a cage.

I didn't ask, but wondered how long I'd be stuck here.

"You'll stay here until I see that you are fit to leave." With those words, she left, leaving me behind bars and alone in the dark.

Days must have passed, but without a window, it proved hard to tell. I became thirstier and thirstier, waiting to be fed. I daydreamed until my mind went dull with boredom. Rage for my mother filled my mind until I felt empty with wrath. Then sadness took the place of emptiness. That sadness slipped into deep depression.

After many lonely hours, the lights came on.

I snapped up, looking. At first, I thought I imagined it. My little sister Cordelia entered the room, her gait short, and she looked nervous. Her eyes were fixed on me, like she approached a lion and feared enraging the beast. Oddly, her hands were behind her back.

Cordelia stopped just out of my reach. "Mother

wanted me to give you this." Cordelia produced a blood bag from behind her back.

My hand lurched out to the bag like a greedy zombie. My sister jumped back while I snatched it. Fear creased her face, which became a mask of horror.

In my frenzied state, I hadn't noticed that Mother entered the room. She towered behind my sister, standing several heads higher. "See what happens to those who disobey me. She is a fool. Do not become her."

"You've not fed her," Cordelia said.

I barely heard her, my thoughts centered on feeding.

My arms extended searching for more blood. *Did she have more?* One hand remained behind her back. I hoped for more. The taste of blood only amplified my thirst.

Cordelia's face reflected pity, as well as fear, when she offered me the second blood bag.

I don't remember draining the bag, but I do recall hearing Cordelia saying something I didn't comprehend while I remained busy draining the last drops.

With the blood bag emptied, Mother said, "You will not be like this, Cordelia. You will be strong. You will be wise. You don't have to like me, but you must understand this is what happens to *fools*."

With that, they left, leaving me alone in the dark.

22. MY PHONE BECOMES MY UNIVERSE

Silence became my friend, the dark and a dull musty smell, my only company. Solitude brought a strange kind of peace, one I'd not felt before. I prayed for hours. Religion, my mother once said, was "rituals and nonsensical stories." Her hatred of religion drew me toward faith growing up.

Occasionally, guards walked me to the bathroom. Even vampires need to go since we drink. But they didn't feed me much, so I didn't need to go often.

Then the light came on. My little sister, Cordelia, stood at the door—her eyes unblinking as if gauging my mental state. "How are you, Alexia?" Cordelia asked.

"I'm fine."

She walked to me, her gaze fixed on me with both hands behind her back, to hide the blood bags. Though not free of the cravings, my time alone helped me gather control. From behind her back she offered me a bag. Her arms extended long to shield herself with distance. I took the blood, careful not to act too crazed. Holding it, I felt a primal blood lust. That must have made us dangerous when our vampire ancestors hunted.

"Alexia, I'm so sorry." Her gaze went away from me towards a plain white wall. The room was bare, but for my cage and a ceiling light.

"Is... Rachel?" I asked between gulps.

"She escaped," she said still averting her gaze.

Draining the blood bag with zeal must make me appear grotesque.

"Good," I gasped. "If I am going to be here a long time, I'd like my cell phone."

"Okay, I'll try to get one. I can't stay long. I gotta go." She left quickly, clearly rattled by the situation.

I often wondered exactly where in Mother's mansion I was. With the absence of windows, I guessed a large closet, otherwise a room in the basement. *This must be Mother's side of the house, since I didn't recognize the room.*

Days passed in darkness, but Cordelia returned. She offered me a blood bag. After I fed, she told me, "I couldn't get your own phone, but I got you a burner. Hide this."

I snatched it and quickly stowed it beneath my

clothes.

A man came to the door, telling her she needed to go.

"Bye. I'll try and get you out." With that, she left.

The phone's clock read 12:33 P.M. I tried texting my friend, Lionel, Felix's older brother. No reply. I texted my boyfriend, Jonathan. No response.

Then I texted Felix.

Me: Hello it's me, Alexia.

Felix: They let you out?

Me: No.

I heard footsteps going down the steps behind the door.

Me: Gotta go

It turned out to be only someone passing by.

After I received the phone, I didn't have long to wait, maybe a day. Cordelia came one last time. One of Mother's soldiers stood nearby.

Cordelia offered me several large blood bags.

I snagged them. For the first time since I was turned, I felt warm. That was more than I had ever consumed at one time up to that point.

"I asked if you could be released as a birthday

present. Mother agreed," Cordelia said

Taking a final gulp. "Released? How long?" I dare not get my hopes up. A man used a key to open my cage.

Cordelia pulled the door open, "Hopefully forever."

23. HAPPY BIRTHDAY

I stared at the pool out the window of my mother's study, the lights in the pool just turned on for the evening.

I'd been free only minutes.

All of the people who worked for our House waited in suits. She deliberately made everyone wait. *Late on purpose, Mother.*

I didn't wish to see my mom so soon after she slammed me into that cage.

The men kept their distance from Cordelia and me. Anne hadn't appeared yet. I wondered if Mother let her go, since Anne didn't need to pretend to be my friend any longer.

"What is the meeting about?" I asked.

Cordelia shrugged and took me to a corner of the

room, "All I know is she said she's going to keep you on a leash, Mom's words. And you can't leave the house."

I put my hand on Cordelia's shoulder. "I doubt that waiting for Mom to make a speech is how you want to spend your birthday."

From outside the mansion, fearful yelling broke out. One of my mother's men yelled, "Man down. North, silencer, in the woods." I gathered the statement meant that a shooter from north of the house had fired with a silencer from the woods. One man may be dead.

We are under attack. Why and from whom?

As my heart rapped in my chest, I fought to look calm.

Cordelia couldn't hear it. The yelling remained out of human range. The guards in the room turned their attention to the sound, even though no window faced the front of the house. The men mumbled among themselves.

Cordelia noticed this and asked, "What's going on?"

I gestured for her to be quiet, as I tried to listen.

Cute Guard said, "We're with your children…" he said into his earphone. Then, to men in the room, "Move out!" The guards sped down the hall, almost at a runner's pace.

Then to us, "Come with me, I have to take you to a safe place."

"What's going on?" Cordelia ask him.

"We are under attack. I'm taking you to a safe room," Cute Guard said.

To my surprise, Cordelia fidgeted, but didn't look more scared by the situation.

The guard took us to a guestroom near our bedrooms, but still on Mother's half of the mansion. I knew our bedrooms to be in the hall on the other side of the wall. He pulled a bookshelf from its place. The books were Harvard Classics and other old books like complete works of Shakespeare. Mother had good taste in books.

He moved the bookshelf, then peeled a panel away, revealing the safe-room.

"Get in," said Cute Guard.

The room's lights turned on as we entered. The guard didn't follow us. At the threshold, he said, "When I put the panel in place, lock it. Do not open it for anyone you don't recognize." He slammed the panel into place. Then I heard the bookshelf being returned with a thud.

24. OPENED TO DARKNESS

The walls to the safe-room were robin's egg blue. Three bland looking beds sat next to separate walls, one for each daughter, me, Cordelia, and Rachel. I guessed that Mother created this room before Rachel ran away. Mother, I felt sure, planned on going to her own safe room. She wouldn't want to be stuck in a room with her own children. She knew us, and herself, better than to want that.

Cordelia appeared much too calm, so I had to ask, "What's going on?"

"Bite me," my sister said. It was a request, not an insult.

"What?"

"The attack is a distraction. This is Rachel's plan. We have to go through the house to leave. So bite me, so no bleeding vampire will hurt me."

"Whoa. Rachel's been talking to you?"

"No, but Felix has forwarded messages to me."

"And her plan is to attack the House?" I asked.

"Yes, with the help of an unnamed House. Rachel said she couldn't tell me, but from what Mom has taught me, I suspect the House to be Byron." Then she added, "You have to bite me."

"I can't turn you."

"Yes, you can. You've been thirstier than even a newly turned vampire. Rachel noticed that when you were at the motel. Your thirst is high because you can turn someone. I fed you several bags. It'll be enough."

"But wouldn't I have an urge to bite another human, if that's the case?"

"That's part of the reason you were in the cage. You're on the tail end of that period, so the urge is all but gone. So bite me," Cordelia said.

"No. If someone is attacking the house, can't we wait for them to win, if that's Rachel's plan?"

"It's just a distraction. We have about a ten-minute window, if that. Bite me."

"*No.* You will turn when your vampire side takes over naturally. Not by me, not by anyone." Then I added as I looked around the room for a plan, "We are getting out of here."

Could there be another entrance to the safe room? If I'm right, we are next to Rachel's unused bedroom. It made sense to have the safe room by the eldest daughter. Mother may have wanted the eldest to protect the younger siblings. Rachel was born to be Mother's right-hand. I looked to the other bookshelf opposite of the door we came through. Old paperbacks of *Harry Potter*, the *Twilight* saga, and Robert Heinlein novels lined this shelf. The bookshelf started to budge, and I removed a panel that opened to darkness.

"Where is this?" Cordelia said, gazing into the black.

I smelled dust. The room remained silent and dark. My vampire eyes should have been able to pick up *some* light. The lightlessness suggested it didn't even have windows.

To my sister, "Stay here."

Gunfire went off in the distance.

Using my hands, I fumbled for a light near the threshold. I stepped into the dark room and felt my way in. My hands found clothes on hangers to each side of me. I followed down the line of clothes on hanging racks to either side.

From the size of the room, this is a walk-in closet.

At the end, I discovered a light switch about where it would be in my closet. The light switched on; I looked down to Cordelia who peered through from the safe room. "This is Rachel's room," I said, now that I knew for certain.

My sister stepped in.

I opened the door to a dusty bedroom.

Gunfire boomed in the front yard. *I can't take Cordelia downstairs, wounded vampires may smell her.*

I opened the door to the balcony, and stepped out, calculating my next move. My sister came with me, first looking down at the pool, then to me.

"Love you, sis," I said. She looked perplexed for a split second, then I grabbed her and tossed her over the balcony.

Cordelia hit the pool with a splash.

She wiped wet hair from her face and yelled, "This isn't part of the plan."

I perched on the windowsill. "Yeah, I like this one better." I jumped, falling two stories into the pool right next to Cordelia, splashing her hard.

My sister glared at me.

"Happy birthday," I said.

25. POOL PARTY

"Bite me, so no one kills me." My sister looked pathetic in her dress… mad and upset.

"Eternal life is not your birthday present." *I think that's the weirdest thing I've ever said.*

Wet hair covered her narrow, scowling eyes. "You're going to get me killed. I hate you."

I wiped the mascara that ran from her eyes. "No, you are going to be fine. Let's get outta here."

Paddling to the edge, I lifted myself out first. Then, I yanked Cordelia up and out of the pool.

"Look around you. That's a fifteen-foot brick fence. How do we get around it?" my sister said, exasperated and dripping wet.

True, the backyard had a fifteen-foot wall, complete with glass shards on the top. But biting her

113

scared me. I didn't want my sister to become a monster like me.

Gunfire echoed outside.

I ran into the garden. *Getting out might prove impossible.*

"Cordelia!" Mother roared. It sounded like she had roared from the window of Rachel's room.

Splash. Someone fell into the pool.

Cordelia looked at me, her eyes wide. "She's coming for us."

"I know, I'll be ready."

"She'll kill you!"

"No, she won't. I have a plan."

My brain scrambled for one. I darted to the tool shed hidden behind bushes. It looked old and ugly. Mother wanted it out of view of the house. I dashed inside the shed with sister in tow. Snatching a tool from the wall, I shoved it into her hands.

"Use this." I didn't even look to see that I'd given her a hatchet. "Stay here."

Without looking, I snatched something from the tool rack and exited. I closed the shed and spun around, hearing someone yell.

Mother glared at me. She stood wet. My hands

gripped a mallet. "I'll ask again. What are you doing?" Mother yelled.

"Leaving," I seethed. The smell of pool water hung in the air. "*We* are leaving." I walked away from the shed.

Mother took off her high-heeled shoes. How odd that she still had them on, considering she had dove into the pool.

"Then you die." Not anger, but relief hung in her eyes. Now she knew, in her mind, that she had to kill me. That relieved her of any worry.

We both knew that today—after eighteen years—one of us would finally be free of the other. Eighteen years, and I would be free of her.

She picked up one of her shoes. I wondered why. Maybe the heel might be used as a weapon. "Come, Alexia, you're out-matched."

I hold a mallet, but she claims I am out-matched. She's playing games with my mind. No, she knows something I don't.

I darted for her. The heavy weapon slowed me. Her smile grew just as I closed in. With my swing, she spun and hammered her shoe into my back.

She laughed, "Try again." She strutted bare foot near where I had stood by the shed door. Cordelia stood by the door holding her hatchet, her eyes wide and scared. "If you watch your sister die, you'll prove to me you know the difference between fools and leaders." I understood that was meant for Cordelia.

The mallet turned out to be too slow. I held it to the ground and stomped on its handle. My human self might have struggled breaking it. Instead, it broke with an easy snap. Now, I held a lighter weapon with only a pointy end.

My back still ached from Mother's stiletto heel attack.

I needed to hit her this time. This time I needed to make a hit if I was to stand a chance. *I'm going to kill my mother. It will be one of the few truly good things I've done, other than trying to free my sister.*

With my broken mallet handle, I charged. I feinted with the stick and plowed my foot into Mother's stomach. She dropped her shoe and grabbed my weapon; I yanked her to me and bit her face. We both fight for control of my mallet handle.

Mother roars in pain. Cordelia stands behind Mother, and her hatchet stands in the top of Mother's back. But Mother's eyes fixed ahead. "This is your doing."

I thought she meant me, but I followed her gaze to Rachel. Rachel stood with a bloodstained shirt. Her right hand held Cute Guard's head by the hair. She gestured with the head. "This is for making me think he loved me."

I didn't understand the meaning, but I ran as I saw her toss a Molotov cocktail at Mother.

Cordelia and I darted towards Rachel who yelled for us to follow. A ladder stood next to the fence with a sleeping bag laying over the top, covering the glass.

We climbed over the fence and were free.

Once over the fence, I heard a strange, broken voice. "Cordelia," it called.

26. FREE

"I'll lure Mother's men away from you," Rachel said, giving me a hug. We were miles away from home. Lionel and Felix waited in a car.

"No, come with us," I said. Felix and Lionel sat in the car. Cordelia stood behind me. Both Lionel and Felix had all they brought with them in a backpack in the trunk. Cordelia, never being the simple type, managed to smuggle out three rolling suitcases of stuff.

"I'm needed in Vancouver."

Needed in Vancouver. You are a bundle of secrets. "Thanks for everything."

"You're free. No house will bother you. Be the best human you can be. You have to live a long time with the person you've become."

It would be a full year until I saw her again. By

then, I had become a different person. I hope I was the person she wanted me to be.

Part II: Runaways

27. A HIDEOUT: HOME

*For many reasons, I should regret my life. I've run away
from home. People want to kill me, and unlike most teenagers, who
only think their parents are evil, my mother actually is. Despite that,
I know I'm the luckiest runaway on earth. I ran away with friends
and my sister. Though my mother is cruel, she gave me the greatest
gift on earth, immortality. Now I am a vampire.*

I sat on a tree branch ten feet above Felix who
stared up at me. I strapped a camera to the tree branch.

"Alexia, do you think they will find us?" Felix
asked.

I thought about it. "No," I said, if only to comfort
him. It was only a guess.

"Do you think our parents will kill us? I mean for
real?" Felix asked.

His parents seemed relatively sane compared to

my mother. Perhaps they only seemed better. I didn't really know them. "I think our parents loved us. Even vampires are capable of love." *I am anyway.*

I turned the camera on, dropped ten feet with a hard thud, and texted my sister, Cordelia.

Me: Do you see through camera one?

Cordelia: I see you.

Good.

If either a vampire or human snooped on the property, we'd see them.

I walked to another tree. The one thing I noticed right away is that the country is so quiet. Except for birds chirping, there are no persistent sounds. We have no neighbors and only the occasional car passes on this lonely country road.

"Can I do the next one?" Felix started to climb a nearby tree.

I feared he'd get hurt and bleed. I'd just fed on a deer, but it wasn't safe with me around blood. I'm new to fighting the urge. "No, Felix, I don't think that's a good idea."

He didn't argue, but instead smiled and changed the topic. "If only your friends could see you now."

I climbed up, and he tossed me a camera. *Yes, indeed, climbing trees isn't much like the old me. I don't miss my friends as much as I thought. I miss my boyfriend, Jonathan, the most. He's safe. As evil as Mother is, she doesn't have a need to harm him. He knows nothing.*

"Did it hurt?" Felix stared up at me. "Being bitten and turning vampire, I mean?"

Without thinking, I reached for my ankle that dangled from the branch, the scar now gone, thinking back to when Mother hired a person to turn me... *yes, it had.*

* * *

Jonathan sat up, screaming and panting. He looked around, not sure where he was.

It felt like he'd slept on a bed, but not his own. He noticed a pain on his neck. It felt like a bite.

"Greetings, Jonathan," an older female voice called in the dark room.

It took a while for Jonathan's eyes to adjust to the darkness. He barely made out a form that sat only a few feet away. Then he recognized the face, dark hair only long enough to reach the top of the neck. And even in a room lit by an alarm clock, her face looked like a cold emotionless mask. He'd only seen her once before, Alexia's mother, Fiona. "What am I doing here?" He tried to remember. *I was driving home after the football game. There was a woman in the road, I swerved... I crashed and then...and then...* "She bit me."

"Yes, I hired her."

Hired her? "What's going on? Where's Alexia?"

"She ran away." Fiona clenched her tiny fist in the dark. Her club hands laying on the armrest looked pale and cruel against the gentle red glow of the clock. "Did she tell you anything before she left?"

Jonathan's heart pounded. *She must have ran away about when she broke up with me. Why would Alexia do this?* "I don't know anything, Fiona. Have you kidnapped me?"

"Your girlfriend never told you what she really was."

What is she talking about?

"She's a vampire," Fiona said.

Jonathan reached for where he'd been bitten. *That's nonsense. Vampires don't exist, and I've seen Alexia eat— but last time she seemed... different somehow.*

"And now so are you," Fiona stood hovering over Jonathan as he sat up in bed.

"Why are you doing this to me?"

"Because, I've been a bad parent." She paced the dark room. "You know my daughter better than I do. I want you to help me find her."

"Go ask her sister—"

"She ran away, too!" Fiona snarled.

"She never told me anything." *The last time I'd seen*

her on the phone, when she broke up with me, she seemed sad and distant.

Jonathan stood, his body felt like it had gone through a rigorous workout. "I'm not helping you."

"You don't want to leave *yet.*"

"Yeah, I do," Jonathan looked for a door.

"But, you feel thirsty, don't you?"

28. TASER

After installing twenty cameras, I stepped into the house. I heard my younger sister Cordelia upstairs talking to Lionel, Felix's older brother.

"I need a drink after today," Lionel said.

They don't know I can hear them all the way upstairs and behind a door, now that I'm a vampire. Good for me. I'll let her smuggle in alcohol, but they need to be sober. We are in danger.

"Just don't tell," Cordelia said.

"All right, you two come down," I shouted up the stairs.

They rushed down.

Everyone sat around the dining room table. I plunked all the money we possessed on the table for them to see. The pile looked like a lot, but it really wasn't. "Eight thousand dollars… this is the cash Rachel gave us."

"Now, we need to divide the duties. Some jobs will require money, like going to town and getting stuff like ammo for our AR-15s and body armor. We don't have much, so we must spend it wisely. Because even now we're not truly safe."

The other three passed awkward looks at each other. It appeared that all three had talked about something behind my back and now were uncomfortable to say what they discussed.

"Look, I'm not the boss, so if I've made a mistake, tell me," I said.

The two boys, Felix and Lionel, looked at my sister, Cordelia. Apparently, she'd been selected to tell me. "You've done nothing wrong." She gazed at the table while she spoke. "But you're right. *We* aren't truly safe." Cordelia sighed and then fixed her eyes on me. "Look, we've all seen the look you have when it comes close to hunting time. We need Tasers. We don't want …" she looked down "… to risk hurting you more than necessary."

"You're afraid I might kill you?"

Felix's eyes narrowed. He stared downward. "I trust you, Alexia, but we can see it in your eyes. It's hard. You're a newly turned vampire. We need a chance if you lose control."

"I'll try to be careful."

"Yes," Lionel said, "but if you attack one of us,

we want to be able to defend ourselves *without* permanently hurting you."

They're right. This is prudent. "Okay...two-thousand dollars for Tasers." They respected me and feared me. *Great, I'm like my mother, at least a little bit.*

Cordelia snatched the cash.

Now that the topic of money was over, I continued. "Okay now, back to dividing up the duties. I've got the cameras installed, and now we'll need one person watching the cameras at all times."

"Whoa," Cordelia said. "One of us has to stare at the screen all the time? Why can't all of us do that? We have our tablets and computers. Let's do it that way."

"Because if we *all* are supposedly watching them at the same time, then none of us are monitoring them," I said, "everyone will think they're being watched by someone else."

Felix gave a solemn nod.

I continued, "There's a treadmill in the security room. You'll at least be doing something."

"Boring," Cordelia said.

"We're going to need it." I bumped my fist on the table. "We need to see our parents coming."

We divided the schedule for watching the camera feed.

"Okay, moving on, entertainment?"

"That's not a real job," Cordelia said.

That sentiment was fine with me. I didn't want Cordelia in charge of entertainment. She'd plan something crazy. Lionel, I love him, but he has no imagination.

"I want that." Felix shot up his hand.

"You got it," I said, clapping my hands together. *Done! That leaves me time to just… worry about us getting killed.*

Cordelia looked in the fridge. "We don't have much food."

"Lionel, why don't you come with me?" Then, to my sister and Felix, "You two stay here while we are gone."

Since becoming a vampire, I've learned why dogs stick their heads out the car window. Everything hits your senses at about fifty miles per hour. Numerous smells slam your senses, telling you the story of the road in fast-forward. So, as we drove back from the grocery store, I let the wind hit my face.

"You want to stick your tongue out, too?" Lionel asked.

"Cute." There was a reason I took Lionel with me. "Lionel, you smell like a vampire."

He took his gaze off the road… confused.

"It's okay, you've not changed yet. I met a woman at the mall who smelled vampire on me before I turned." I laughed. "I had no idea what she was talking about."

"What should I do?"

"Nothing, you're still a normal human. I'll ask my sister, Rachel, the next time she opens a line of communication." I smelled something outside. "Whoa, stop the car."

The tires snarled on the gravel shoulder of the country road.

"What is it?"

"I smell a vampire and a human."

Lionel tensed. "Oh, no, they found us."

We were still miles from home. "I don't know. I don't recognize their smells. Both the human and vampire haven't washed in days. The vampire is female and the human is male." The unclean smell suggested she wasn't one of Mom's hirelings.

Lionel shook his head. "Alexia, we should go."

"The scent is days old, plus the wind is blowing toward me, so I will know of their presence before they see me. I'll be reasonably safe. We should find our vampire neighbors, if any, before they find us. Maybe the vampire has a home nearby. If so, we must know. Stay here. Lock the car and get the Glock out. I'll follow the smell. Keep the car running, and be ready to peel out just in case." I stepped from the car and followed the smells.

"Do you know if the vampire and human actually crossed paths?" Lionel asked, poking his head out the passenger side window.

"Both scents are just as old. I believe there's a chance they were together."

Lionel clutched his Glock. "Should I at least go with you?"

"No, you're not turned; it's not safe."

I followed the smell that crossed a gravel road then led to a dirt path. A pair of boot prints had pressed into the sun-cracked mud.

Behind me, the car engine stopped and the door clunked open. Over my shoulder, I saw Lionel mouth, "I'm not leaving you." So I whispered for him to stay far behind me.

He nodded.

We both followed the earthen path in silence. Lionel stayed ten yards behind.

I didn't see two pairs of shoe prints, just one in the mud. If they walked this way, why only one set? I compared the prints with my own, they were both larger and wider than mine, likely a male's print. The female's scent hovered lower, like she stood at about a tween's height. *The vampire is either very short or very young.* She walked the shoulder of the path in the grass, like she didn't want to get her shoes dirty in the mud.

That's right, we'll live forever, but we'll be damned if we get our shoes muddy.

Then, ten strides away, a smaller shoe print. I compared my foot size to it. She appeared to be small, meaning she was young, perhaps.

Ahead stood a modest two-story home. Paint peeled from its mud-splattered walls. I guessed both floors might be just a bit larger than my bedroom back home. In the front lawn, I spotted a burned out bonfire. A lazy stream of smoke slithered into the blue sky. The bonfire was made of tree limbs of odd shapes and sizes, giving the look of a giant singed bird's nest.

The scent of both the vampire and human thickened just ten feet before the tree line. A heavier smell meant they likely stood there for a few minutes. No indication of violence. *Did they talk?*

The little vampire had veered off the path into the woods. The human then continued along the path. I followed the vampire's smell to the edge of the woods. She stayed there long enough for her scent to be stronger, maybe fifteen minutes. She waited at the edge of the tree line with the house in view. *Why? What did she wait for?*

I returned to the trail of the human. I knew he'd likely be dead or turned, but I felt I needed to know.

I'm not my mother. I look out for others.

His scent continued in the field going toward a

house. *Is this a vampire coven?*

I followed the man's scent.

An acrid smell hit my nose. The vampires had burned something in the bonfire. My heart stopped halfway to it. A pale skull stared from blackened wood and tendrils of smoke. *This is not a bonfire, but a pyre!*

The smell of vampires and the man hovered over the scene of horror. I wondered how the human died. Six skulls filled the pyre. A few singed strands of hair clung to their skulls, offering a glimpse of life now gone. Blackened and tattered clothes wrapped bones and charred flesh. White gels hung like icicles to sticks near the bones; I guessed it to be human fat. That acrid smell of burnt flesh smothered the air.

The pyre only compounded my confusion. It seemed clear the human was burnt here, but clearly some vampires were killed. *More strange, I smell six vampires and there are six skulls. One of them must have survived. Did they fight over the human like a pack of dogs? The little vampire scent is not here. Did she watch what happened? She must have remained in the forest and ran.*

Lionel stood at the tree line. *He might see my fear. I must be brave. I'm taking the lead into this new life.* I gestured for him to stay.

The front door of the house stood ajar.

The living room couch skewed at an odd angle to the wall mounted television that lay face down; nearby, a single shoe sat without an owner. A wall clock lay ticking on the floor. Drops of blood contrasted against the white walls and white tiled floor. I looked for signs of life. None.

The vampires did live here. My sense of smell let me know they once lived here for a while. The human was the newcomer. The little girl lived here a short while, but didn't return to the fight.

A cellphone buzzed in the kitchen, it said someone named Madison called.

Lionel walked into the house with his gun, his face pale, his gaze lurching left and right. I heard his heart rapping from ten feet away. He looked frightened. I felt scared, too.

A thudding sound from upstairs snapped my attention away. With it, a gasping breath.

Halfway up the stairs, I passed a broken railing. The human scent thickened, as if nearby. I didn't have much hope that he had lived.

I gasped. The man lay at the landing. His eyes stared blankly, but he still breathed. Bites covered his skin like leopard spots. The different sizes of bite marks showed many vampires bit into him.

Why is he the only survivor?

"It doesn't make sense," Lionel said. "How did *he* survive all this?" Lionel gestured in the direction of the vampire skulls outside.

I wondered that myself. *Why did the weakest person, a human, survive a vampire battle?* "Those horrible creatures."

"Alexia, you *are* one of those creatures."

I nodded. No argument there. *But could I ever be violent or evil like that?*

Lionel stepped closer. "What do we do?" He looked to me for an answer.

I looked at the fallen man. *Leave him and be guilty of what happens because I did nothing? No. I am raising my sister to be better than Mother. And sometimes that starts with a hard choice.* "We take him."

29. TRUTH

In my hundreds of years, I have learned many things that humans would find repugnant. The truth scares the young, and all humans are young. My eldest daughters, Rachel and Alexia, feel that way about the truth. I have hope for Cordelia, though her older siblings have beguiled her. I can forgive her for being young and fooled by those who claim to love her. I can teach her the true ways of the world.

Lying is often the best way to speak with others. To tell the truth often means surrendering too much. In this case I will make fools of the Ruthvens. They pretend nothing is wrong. I know that their children, Lionel and Felix, have run away with my daughters. Their pretensions are something I can exploit.

The two walk in. They hide it, but I know they're nervous, wondering if this has to do with their wayward children. Ellen, the wife, has a spray tan. Really, a spray tan? I can understand trying to fit in and hide who you are, but getting sprayed with chemicals, ugh.

Eric Ruthven is bald on top and can't get hair plugs

because vampire skin is really tough. He's looking to have custom equipment made for hair plugs. Their outfits are behind the times. I warned them to be mindful of fashion.

"How are your children?" I asked.

Their eyes narrow, they don't hide their anger well. They wonder, what game is she playing?

"Fine," the mother said.

I laugh. Not a happy one... a bitter one. I keep it going for ten seconds. Their faces hint of helpless anger. "I thought we were not going to lie to each other," I say, with a hint of a smile.

"Fiona," Eric said, "What are you talking about?"

I looked to the wife, Ellen, to see if she wished to continue playing this game. She remains silent. *Very well. Feigning ignorance is a bad play. They are only allowing me to taunt them.*

"Well, your children were here just a few weeks ago."

They shifted uncomfortably in their seats. *They let their pride take advantage of them. One must admit to defeat.* "Your two sons came to my house, and they did this." With those words, I jerked my sleeve up to expose my right arm. They saw the burns and gasped.

"We don't know where they are," Eric protested.

"They ran away with Alexia's help," I said. "This

is our problem. We need to cover this up, or we will look like failures. Rumors spread fast and may have already started. We will work as a team to find our wayward children before they further humiliate *both* of our houses."

"We need a lead, some information about where they might be hiding," Ellen said.

"I have… recruited help."

The Ruthven's did not ask. They merely nodded, confident that I knew what I was doing.

I did not even ask them to help. To ask would be to invite them to make a choice. They had played the meeting badly by denying trouble. This meeting worked very well for me.

* * *

Jonathan hated his new life. His transformation left him weak. He hurt all over. He hated Alexia for abandoning him, for leaving him in the dark about what was going on. He hated her because that was all he had left.

Someone knocked at the door.

"What?"

"It's me." Anne stood at the threshold. "May I come in?"

Before turning, Jonathan knew Anne only as Alexia's friend. Now he understood she worked for Fiona, but for what purpose remained unclear.

Anne took a seat on a cushioned wooden chair. "Did Alexia ever tell you about the shrink she had in middle school?"

Jonathan shook his head.

"What Alexia didn't know was that the shrink's ultimate purpose was to get an understanding of her. Fiona hired her because she needed to understand her daughter. She is too cold and too distant to truly know her daughters."

"Why are you telling me this?"

"Because Fiona is a terrible mother, those are her words. Now she needs your help to get her two children back. I was supposed to watch Alexia and make sure she didn't run away like Rachel. If you don't help me find her," she whispered her next words, "Fiona will kill me."

Alexia, why did you leave me to this? You sold me out, and I loved you. "Where do we start?"

30. SLEEPER

Cordelia looked horrified as I brought in the bitten man. Lionel helped open the door. As a human, he is strong, but as a vampire, I'm stronger.

Confusion and fear crossed the faces of Felix and Cordelia. We should have called to warn them before we arrived.

"Can you guys get the groceries from the trunk? I'll carry him to my room." We had no guestroom, and I figured I was the one who brought him, so I should give up my bed.

I can't describe the feeling of watching a man die. The bitten man seldom moved, and always had a sheen of sweat on his skin. He had no wallet, no ID, just a bag of marble-sized stones in his pocket.

Rachel's phone number no longer worked. She hadn't contacted me, and I really needed her.

"You know he's unlikely to turn," Felix said, popping his head in the door that I had left ajar. By the time we found him, he'd been lying there for a day. Rachel said we could only turn people at certain times.

"But there's a chance," I said, looking down at the now sleeping man.

Felix nodded as he walked in.

"He deserves a chance," I said.

Felix crossed his arms. "The only thing for certain is that he's in pain... and it's likely he'll die. I don't think they bit him to turn him. From what you described of the place, it seems he fought them, Alexia."

"What if no one is there when he wakes up?" Cordelia asked.

"Don't worry," I said, as I fanned my hands. "When we first turn, we are too weak to harm anyone. Felix, watch him, and be ready. I will need to go hunt soon. Otherwise, when I'm here, I'll know if he wakes up."

My sister crossed her arms and narrowed her eyes. "Will you?"

"Yes. I can hear your heart beat now. All vampires have good hearing."

"Oh, yes." Felix smiled. "You asked me to think of something we could do to pass the time. I've got an idea, Dungeons and Dragons."

Felix must have seen my expression change.

"No, no, don't judge until you try it. Vin Diesel played it."

I may have used poor judgment in putting him in charge of entertainment. But, I've other things to worry about. Like what to drink? Vampires normally need to feed once a week, but I'm getting thirsty twice a week. Could something be wrong with me?

I walked out of the house, enjoying the sun and the large open field. I spotted a rabbit three yards from the tree line. It didn't see me, yet. A rabbit wouldn't be much to drink, but it's convenient.

I ran. Vampires can sprint twenty-five miles per hour, like Olympic sprinters. The rabbit froze. Perhaps it hoped I hadn't actually noticed it. I closed in. It darted towards the woods. *If it made it there, it'll be able to run around the trees and escape.* I snatched it, rolling with the rabbit locked in my hands.

Standing, second thoughts crept in. It's such a cute creature. The rabbit's heart drummed in its tiny chest while I held it helpless in my grip. *I don't want to become a monst—*

"Ouch!"

It bit me! I dropped the rabbit, and it darted away.

I am the worst vampire, ever!

My phone buzzed, someone had texted me. I looked around, one of the cameras faced me. *Cordelia has gotta be watching.*

Cordelia: Maybe you should try something more helpless… like squirrels or bugs ☺.

I hope she didn't record that.

Cordelia: I recorded it too ☺.

Great. I'm a vampire and yet my little sister still teases me. With a bit of my pride chipped away, I skulked into the woods, looking for something to bite.

An hour later, I walked back home after I snagged a deer. As I stepped into the clearing, I received a text.

Felix: He woke up… sort of

Me: ?

Felix: found him on the stairs all passed out… he must have stumbled out of bed.

I ran to the door where Felix met me. "No one heard him move. I left to get something, but I didn't go far. I should have heard him."

I went to the room where the man lay peacefully, the sweat now gone from his skin. If his many bites weren't visible, I might have thought him a normal person just sleeping.

"He's getting better, and he's not turning pale." Felix's eyes narrowed, and he leaned against the wall,

"What have we brought in?"

Felix is right. He's not turning and he's recovering. What is going on?

31. FINDINGS

I saw the reluctance in Jonathan's eyes. He must hate Alexia as much as he loves her. I need to use that emotion if I am to get out from under Fiona's axe.

Still weak from turning, he managed to sit up in bed. Fiona hadn't let him out of the room yet.

"She left you, Jonathan, and now I need your help," I said.

"Anne, where have they looked so far?" Jonathan grumbled, sitting up a bit straighter.

"Among the smaller covens in the cities. We've inquired mostly in the northwest."

Jonathan shook his head, "You know her better than that. From what you've taught me about vampire culture, Fiona's men are thinking like vampires. Alexia still thinks like a human, and she likes to be the queen bee.

She's not going to make ties to other covens. She *ran* from vampires. She's going to hide out in the country. There, she is harder to find and she doesn't have to see other vampires. In a rural area, she will be in control."

Jonathan is smart. Fiona did well in turning this boy. His conclusions sound correct, but that made looking for her even harder. "That's a lot of ground to travel."

"Maybe, maybe not. She wants to be in an area she knows, even if it's a place she never stayed very long."

"Really, you know her *that* well." I paced by his bed, thinking about what this meant. *Where would she go? Cannon Beach and Astoria? Alexia and I have both been there. She went with me to Lewis County to collect antiques once. She thought I was weird to get "old dead people things." Little did she know I was collecting things from my own lifetime. Yes, add Lewis County to the list.* "Thanks, Jonathan. Your ideas just may have saved me."

32. DUNGEONS AND VAMPIRES

The last thing I remember is killing vampires. I burned their bodies so they didn't come back. I wasn't sure they'd stay dead if I didn't. With the venom overwhelming me, I tried to find a place to rest. Instead, I fell on the landing of the stairs. I'm not sure how long I'd lain there when people found me. I heard them talk while I slept. The girl's name was Alexia.

I awoke. *The room is cleaner than the coven I'd fought in. If they're human, then why hadn't they brought me to a hospital? If they're vampires, why can't I feel their presence like before?*

I need to get out of here.

I felt weak, either from the blood loss or recovery from the many wounds.

My muscles hurt as I sat up. I looked at the teeth marks lining my arms; each hurt like uneven circles of fire.

Downstairs, laughter roared. It sounded like three

people having a good time.

Five painful minutes passed putting on my shoes. With them on, I grabbed the headboard of the bed to stand. My muscles ached with every movement. I lacked the strength to walk quietly, but the constant chatter below made it unlikely anyone heard me.

Stumbling to the wall, I leaned against it for support. With my hand holding the threshold, I exited the room. I headed downstairs... each step made by gripping the railing.

On my trip down the stairs, I overheard the weirdest conversation.

"Wait, wait, this book says that vampire's burn under the sun. That's not realistic. Alexia doesn't burn," said a young female. "Do you, sis?

I recognized Alexia as the one who carried me out of the house. But what are they talking about?

"No. Well, I can probably get sunburned," Alexia sounded a bit older than her sister.

"See," the young sister said.

"It's just a game, Cordelia; we'll play it by the rules," said a young male voice.

"But, Felix, it says here you can *change* the rules," said Cordelia.

It sounds like people arguing about the realism of a game, maybe Dungeons and Dragons, with a real vampire; how did my life get so weird? I pondered, while being careful not to make the steps creak.

"There's THAC0 in this right?" said Alexia.

THAC0, so it's definitely Dungeons and Dragons.

"No, that's another edition," said Felix. "You've played this before?"

"No, a boy who tutored me in—"

"Oh, go figure," said Felix.

Thump.

"*Ow,*" Felix moaned.

She's a vampire with human friends. The others know she's a vampire. They feel safe with her, strange. Weirder still, women outnumber the men playing Dungeons and Dragons. I grunted, going down another step.

Though Alexia is a vampire, I didn't sense her. Maybe she hasn't fed recently. There is so much I don't understand about my new abilities.

"I can't believe the instruction manual is this big," said Alexia.

"Can I be a vampire?" asked Cordelia.

Alexia chuckled, "Not until you're older."

"I meant in the *game,*" the sister laughed.

She chuckled and said, "I know what you meant."

I made it to the middle step. I spied below that the open threshold of the dining room, which offered a clear view of my exit, the front door. From my angle, I spotted only the boy. He stood by a dining table. He had chocolate brown hair and round glasses.

The most nerdish conversation I ever heard continued. "Okay, so if there are other editions, right? Like second, third or maybe fourth, if there is one?" Cordelia asked.

"*Don't* get me started on fourth edition," said the young man.

"I'll check on him," Alexia said. I knew "him" meant me. My heart raced, but I lacked the strength to run.

She stepped into the living room. The girl appeared about eighteen years of age, attractive, with skin just slightly pale. Her eyes widened, as if surprised to see me awake. She fidgeted and stepped back, perhaps nervous.

"You kept us waiting. How do you feel?" Alexia said.

I didn't answer her. She didn't act like a vampire to me. That is, I saw no malice in her eyes. Rather, she seemed kind. *Killers aren't nervous, not the ones I've met. But she might be dangerous.*

"We won't hurt you," she said, stepping closer.

"Stay out of my way," I said, gripping the rail, trying to remain standing.

Her head tilted to one side as she whispered, "Please stay."

Strength drained from me, and I slumped to the third step from the bottom. I winced when she walked up and put a cool hand on my shoulder.

"What is your name?" Her brow knitted.

"Robert, Robert Neville," I lied.

Alexia's sister, Cordelia, walked in and said, "Felix says if I'm to play a vampire I should still burn under the sun."

The young girl froze at the sight of me. Her mouth dropped open, her eyes unblinking. Unlike her older sister, she wasn't pale.

"Are you feeling thirsty?" Alexia asked.

"Kind of," I nodded

Her forehead furrowed, my words must have bothered her.

"Who are you people?" I asked, looking left and right at the two ladies.

"Friends. We're gonna help you get better."

"Why didn't you take me to a hospital?" I scooted down to the next to last step.

She knelt, looking into my eyes. "We knew that was a bad idea considering your— condition."

"*What* are you?" Fatigue overwhelmed me, so I leaned my head against the railing. My eyelids felt heavy.

I saw the gears in her eyes spinning as if she searched for an answer. "Like I said, a friend."

My eyes weighed even more. As I faded out, I remained unsure if I was in danger.

33. MADISON

Robert Neville, leaned on the railing of the stairs, passed out.

Cordelia sighed and said, "Alexia, what kind of person survives that many bites."

"I don't know." *He's not a vampire and still, apparently, human. But wouldn't that much venom kill him? When I was bitten, I felt it burn inside of me. I don't know, so many questions.*

Once again, I wished I had Rachel's guidance. Something like this must have happened before. *What does it mean?*

With that, I carried Robert Neville upstairs, alone.

After the Dungeons and Dragons game, I looked in on Robert Neville. He remained asleep and appeared to be on the mend. Yet, I didn't dare raise my hopes. The man may still die, but I remained firm that we'd help him.

Then, after looking in on him, I searched for Cordelia. Knocking on her door, I received no answer. In the dining room, I asked Felix who was collecting our character sheets for the game. "Where did Cordelia go?"

"Don't know for sure," Felix said, putting all the papers in one of his rule books.

Then I quietly listened for everyone around me. I thought I heard something on the roof. *Is that where she's been hiding?*

I went out on the balcony that wrapped around the second floor. One of my favorite things is the view overlooking the field around the house. Below, the young forest stood around our field, mostly a line of red alders. They weren't pretty trees. White blotches spotted their grey trunks, resembling clouds. Red Alders got their name from the red sap in their trunks. Not a touch of red on them. Despite their bland appearance, I liked the green wooded view.

I walked the balcony until I was just outside Cordelia's room. My sister's scent, mixed with her favorite soap, hovered in the air. Also, a ladder leaned against the wall. *I'd been looking for that ladder.*

As I peered over the edge of the roof, my sister sat waving to me. She didn't seem happy to see me. Maybe she wanted this to be her hiding place. Beside her lay a backpack. I knew it contained alcohol.

All over our roof, green patches of moss dotted the black shingles.

"Mind if I join you," I asked.

She frowned, but said, "Sure," anyway.

"Thanks. I promise I'll let this be your place," I said, taking a second to hop and pull myself up. Cordelia's eyebrows rose as I climbed up on the roof.

"Up here you do have an enviable view," I said, sitting by her side.

Felix opened the French doors to his room, "Where are you guys?"

"Up here," Cordelia said, calling down from the roof.

Felix's eyes widened, looking excited. "Can I join you?"

"Sure, I guess this is everyone's hideout now," my sister said.

I felt bad. My baby sister likes to tuck herself away from people sometimes. Now that we are on the run, it's hard to be alone. The woods aren't safe if people are looking for us.

Felix hopped to the ladder and shot right up.

"I think the Dungeons and Dragons game went well," Felix said, sitting next to me and putting me in the middle between them.

"Well," Cordelia said, "a little unrealistic. Vampires are undead in that game. Alexia's not dead."

True. But I found myself checking my pulse anyway. *Yup, still there.*

"Ugh, I don't think anyone has ever argued about the game's realism before," Felix said.

"I'm sure I'm not the only one," Cordelia shot back.

"Really?" Felix said.

"I'm sure vampires have. And I bet they corrected the rule about burning under the sun."

"Not that again," Felix said, crossing his arms.

I wondered if poor Robert Neville had heard our conversation when he climbed down the stairs during our game.

"Look, about Robert Neville. I know he might pose a danger, but we need to remain good people. We must protect him. That's something I want you to look into, Felix. See what you can find out about this man."

"Right," Felix said, pecking at his phone, apparently already searching.

Lionel paged me.

Lionel: X

That meant people are coming. Cordelia and Felix

looked at their phones too. He had paged everyone.

Lionel: 1 Car. No Gun.

Since the coven nearby had been razed, we stayed on even higher alert. Lionel didn't see a gun, but for now we'd assume they were just hiding it.

I dropped off the roof, as did Felix. Cordelia went down the ladder.

Everyone grabbed a weapon from the security room. We had planned this out and each of us played their role. Cordelia took a sniper rifle. Felix had an AR-15 but watched the cameras from the security room and informed her of any targets in the woods and fields. Felix only left the security room if there were too many near the house, and we needed another shooter. Lionel took an AR-15 and hurried to the first floor with me. All of us had a shotgun strapped over our shoulders for close combat.

I said over the phone to everyone, "Just remember, this could be a harmless human or curious vampires. Keep your weapons ready if it's not. And keep them hidden."

I watched a single cherry-red 1970's car drive up the gravel road with only one occupant, a female in her late teens or early twenties. The car door opened and a girl trotted out of the car. She had thick blonde hair that almost reached her elbows.

I shook my head. *I don't think she drove here to attack us.*

She walked to the door and knocked.

Maybe she's a neighbor. Or maybe she's looking for a quartet of runaway half-vampires. I walked to the door. "Hello?"

"Hi, my name is Madison," she said.

I remembered Madison's name from the phone where we found Robert Neville. I doubted the name coming up twice was a coincidence.

"Hi, I'm Alexia. How are you?" I stepped out. I needed to keep her way from the smells of the others, since they were all human.

"You got this place from Rachel?"

I nodded, kicking the heads of dandelions that grew in the field. "Yes, we are like family."

"Any friend of Rachel's is a friend of mine." Madison's eyebrows perked up. She followed me while I walked further into the field where the smell of humans might be less. "Are you aware of what happened to a nearby coven?"

"Yes, I heard about it." I didn't want to get into details, being that we saved a human from the fallen coven. "What happened?"

Madison shrugged, "That's what I'd like to know."

"I didn't know them well, did you?" Madison asked.

I stopped walking and shook my head. "No."

"Well, I can't stay long. But you *must* visit us some time. I run an inn for vampires in Olympia. Need a job with any of the houses, I know about them." She wrote something on a piece of receipt paper.

We said bye to each other, and then she was gone.

My heart still raced as she drove away. I unfolded the paper revealing a North Olympia address. *Who is she?*

34. MADISON AVENUE

"I'm going," I said, looking at Madison's invitation that lay on the dining room table.

"Alexia, this is a bad idea." Cordelia's eyes narrowed, and she crossed her arms. It angered her that I considered the invitation. All around me, people argued I shouldn't go, everyone but Lionel.

Yet he frowned, standing across the table from me. "Fine. But I'm going with you."

"You might smell like a vampire, but you're still human. You've not fully turned yet."

"I know, but you said we need to stick together to survive. You can't have it both ways."

I realize Lionel was smart for a jock.

"Wait, wait," Felix said, "why not make an excuse not to go? We don't need the attention. We just started to hide. Let's keep a low profile, and she'll forget about us."

He had a point. "Yes, Felix, exposure to other

vampires might increase the risk of getting caught. But Madison already found us, and it might be good to make allies where we can. We might need to hide out at someone else's coven eventually.

Cordelia shook her head, "I still think it's stupid."

"I know it's risky." I held up my hands. "But before I—we—left our family homes, I knew that huddling down and hoping that our families don't find us was not the whole answer. I don't want to meet with vampires. But meeting them gives us things we don't have."

Felix crossed his arms. "Like?"

To my surprise, Cordelia answered for me, "More knowledge about local vampires."

"And?" I asked.

"Knowledge of our culture," Felix added.

"Huh?" I asked, confused. *That was a weird answer.*

"*If* we are going to be among our kind, we don't want to embarrass ourselves. So knowing our culture is important." Felix said.

"Wow, that's really good, Felix," I said, "But I was going to go with maybe hearing news from the vampire world in general. Especially if our families have put out an APB on us."

The next day, Lionel and I drove to Madison's coven. She lived in Olympia's commercial district. Coffee shops, head shops, hippies, and hipsters abounded, even a few dreary secondhand bookstores. We asked for directions to the street she lived on. One person called the apartment complex "Meth Heights". I wondered why it had that name, but didn't ask. Madison lived on the top floor.

We found the place eventually. Lionel tapped my shoulder and pointed to a plasma donation center on the first floor of "Meth Heights." A tweaker-ish looking man walked out, munching on a cookie. My sister did say that many modern vampires lived off blood donations.

"Nervous?" Lionel asked a minute later while we climbed up the stairs in "Meth Heights." The elevator was broken.

"Yeah." *How could I not be?* Madison seemed nice, but she's a vampire. I had no idea what I was walking into.

"Don't worry, this is going to work out." Lionel huffed and puffed. Being human, he had less stamina. That was nice of him to say, but I smelled fear on him.

We made it to the top floor. I knocked. Footfalls padded to the door.

"Hello." Madison smiled, opening up. "Come in." She appeared happy to see us. "Forgive the mess. I always try to clean, but I have to fight with everyone else who doesn't care."

It wasn't too messy really, a single t-shirt lay on the living room couch. But a man lay on the couch, apparently asleep.

Something odd snatched my attention. No normal human home would have most of the walls plastered with graffiti art. It appeared to be by the same artist, as the talent remained high throughout the span of the living room. To the creator's credit, it *was* art. To add to the avant-garde image of the living room, an elegant crystal chandelier hung about fifteen feet above us.

"Oh, you're looking at Skip's work," Madison said to me with a proud smile.

"Skip did all of this?" I asked, not sure who Skip was.

"Yes," Madison said. She gestured over her shoulder to a guy with an Afro spraying the wall of the hallway.

Isn't using spray paint in a closed-in area bad for your lungs? Oh wait, we're vampires, sans Lionel anyway.

Skip snapped to his feet, wiped his hand with a rag, and then shook our hands, "Nice to meet you guys." He gestured to the left at the guy lying on the couch. "That's Slick, we *did* tell him you guys were coming, but he shot up anyway."

It took me a split second to get the meaning of "shot up". *He's a heroin addict. The regal stereotype of vampires be damned.*

Skip said to Lionel, "I'll show you around."

Lionel followed Skip down the hall. I worried for Lionel. *Can he pull off being a vampire?*

"Who are these people?" asked a boy in his late teens who shuffled down a hallway. He wore sweat pants and a white t-shirt. A large head and fat lips topped his skinny frame.

"I told everyone the new coven was visiting," Madison said.

"No, no one told me," he whined.

"Be gone, Skeeter." Madison's gaze bored into his eyes.

Skeeter crept off. *Wow, he's annoying.*

"I'll show you my place," Madison said.

Tall windows shed yellow evening light into Madison's room. A wardrobe stood at the back with clothes oozing out of the open door. A large mirror haloed by light bulbs stood at the head of a makeup table. The bed and the floor were neat, but for the already mentioned clothes and a well-ordered stack of magazines.

"Who is in charge of this coven?" I asked.

"I am, it's been that way for a few years now," she said.

"Do the royals leave you alone?" I asked, taking in the view of the street ten floors below.

"Unlike most rogues, we are affiliated with the

royal houses. If vampires, especially ones working for royals, want to stay in one of our rooms below, we provide that. Also, we get the word out about hirings from the big families."

Rogues must mean vampires not part of powerful Houses. That's me too, I guess. "So this coven is a community bulletin board?"

"Yeah."

"So how long has your coven been around?" I asked.

"Good question, we really don't know. This coven has been around a century maybe. None of us are its original members. People, they come and go from this coven. Hey, you wanna try things on? I got clothes from *way* back."

She had quite a collection, even if some of it was in a pile. "I'm getting another wardrobe. A girl's gotta have some material vices, right?"

Against my wisdom, I started to like her. Yet, I wondered how often she hunted people.

"If you want to borrow anything, go right ahead. I've got more clothes than I can honestly wear," Madison said, pressing a blouse against me as if to see how it might look.

She had good taste. The style appeared reminiscent of other decades, which one I wasn't sure, early 90s or 80s. *Not the 70s, well, there's a hint at a punk esthetic.*

"How old are you?" I asked.

Her mouth went to the side. She paused while her eyes went to the left corner. "Including my human years, enough to be old."

"I guess even a vampire girl never tells her age."

"Yeah," she laughed. "And you? I know, I know, I didn't answer your question, but I really gotta wonder."

"I'm nineteen," I said.

"But how long have you been nineteen?"

"Since my birthday."

"But minus your human years, how old are you?"

"Eight months," I said, holding up a blouse and looking in the mirror.

She blinked rapidly and said, "Whoa. You're young. I'm old enough to be your grandmother. But I'm younger, I was turned at seventeen."

I asked to borrow a pink blouse, and she agreed.

"Have you tried the sex offender registration list? We use it when the donations downstairs are short," she asked.

"What?" I had no idea what she spoke of.

"A girl's gotta drink," Madison said. I realized she

asked about feeding.

"Never thought of that."

"So not to pry, but how do you feed?"

Should I say I feed on deer? Oh, and I hope she never hears of the rabbit incident. A quick truth and lie came to me. "Don't like feeding on people, but when I do, it's drug addicts."

Her jaw dropped, "Hardcore!" She clapped her hand on her mouth. "You like the secondhand high, don't you?"

"What can I say, a girl's gotta drink." *I'm such a liar.*

We both laughed. Hers sounded like an honest laugh. I hoped mine didn't sound too nervous.

I'm lying, and I know little about my own culture. When will she find out I'm a phony?

I asked to use the bathroom. Contrary to myth, vampires do use the restroom. My people eat if only for the joy of doing so. But even if we don't eat, we drink blood, and that still has to go somewhere.

I checked the time; my phone read 10:00. *How time has flown. If I like it or not, Madison is becoming a friend. At least, I feel like we are becoming friends. I may need to learn from her; she has acquired more experience at being a coven leader than I.*

I guessed Madison's second birth era, that is, the decade she became a vampire, to be the 80s. That might explain the music she played, and the black and neon colors she favored.

The bathroom door swung open, and a large old man came out. He smelled like a vampire. The man stood inches away from me, clad in a wife-beater, blue jeans, and a belt. His head sported a widow's peak of black hair that hadn't seen a comb, and large brown eyes brimmed with menace.

"Hi." He sounded ambivalent, stepping out of the bathroom.

"Hello," I said.

"You must be from the new coven." The guy's eyes narrowed.

"Yes, I am." I laughed nervously. *Madison is the coven leader with this menacing guy in the group? From the vibe he gave off, he meant trouble. How does she manage? Apparently, she does, since she's on top of the heap.*

On the way back from the restroom, I spotted another member of Madison's coven. Through a door that stood ajar, I spied a light-skinned girl, pale even for a vampire. She sat cross-legged on her bed, apparently, listening to music with headphones. A piercing looped her lip, and below her bed was a sea of stuff, mostly clothes. The one wall I glimpsed streamed with writing jotted in black marker. She's the only other girl I'd seen, except Madison.

Though Madison appeared friendly, I still needed

to size up the group as a potential threat. *There are seven members of this coven that I counted. The greasy kid lying on the couch, who started to stir when I passed by. Skeeter, who was sulking around somewhere, and Skip the artist. The girl in the room listening to music, and some man talking on his phone that I only heard. There's the menacing guy I met at the bathroom door, and finally, Madison, my new friend. I'm getting the vibe that this is a disorganized band of vampires, nothing that might threaten my coven, but maybe the mean-looking man at the bathroom door.*

When I returned to Madison's room, she said, "Let's see what your friend and Skip are up to."

We found Skip and Lionel on the rooftop of the building. The two sat on a couch under the stars. Skip laughed at something Lionel said that I didn't hear. Beside the couch sat an icebox full of beer. Below us shone a view of Olympia, with the city's windows glittering in the dark.

The balmy summer air made the night feel sleepy and relaxed. I couldn't legally drink, but when you are among vampires, things like this can be overlooked, right? Honestly, I'd not taken the drinking laws seriously as a human anyway.

I sat between Skip and Lionel. The couch had seen its better day, its fake leather showing worn spots all over. Oddly, with the fake plants shouldering the couch and the city lights, the sofa possessed personality.

"So, I'll tell you, too." Skip stood and paced before the couch. "I was just telling your friend how to live as a rogue."

"Great," I said.

"So, you gotta live in seven-year increments. People will notice you're not getting old. You can maybe stretch it a little longer with people not aging like they used to, but, people are gonna notice."

"Okay," I said.

"Vancouver went legit." Skip took a final swig of his beer, then dunked it in a trash can to the far side of the roof.

I had no idea about Vancouver. Or what he meant by "legit."

Skip continued, "After proving his innocence, the Rogue Prince in Vancouver now has a formal connection with a royal family. The prince doesn't want to give up the coven he formed in the city with the help of his money. Vancouver is rumored to be crawling with spies."

I had no idea about this prince or his innocence. I guess this prince must be common knowledge. *When he said Vancouver went "legit," that must mean having a royal in good standing. And that royal, therefore, is a legitimate arbitrator of law and order. Vancouver is where Rachel is from, and Skip said it was crawling with spies. Was my sister helping me separate from my House a part of something bigger? I know she loves me, but did she get help not only because a house respected her, but because it's part of a bigger plan? Could even the rogue prince be behind my liberty, albeit, indirectly?* "Why is it crawling with spies?"

"The royals loathe direct warfare. And rogue

covens have defeated royal families before. So, royals are more careful not to risk a defeat." Skip held up his hands while he paced. "It is likely that a royal house is helping the Rogue Prince, while others are trying to take him down, but there is a lot we don't know."

"Oh, and the parties in Vancouver are *epic*," Madison said, taking a beer out of the cooler.

"Wow," I said. *My mother seldom had parties. Why did I have to come from a boring House?*

"Rules for hunting," Skip continued. "Don't hunt in your own town. People catch on and see things, especially with mobile phones having cameras these days. Furthermore, check to see local news of an area. People get careless, Highway 16 in Canada and Nome, up in Alaska, are both examples of vampires being careless and over hunting. Last, don't take human friends home. You never know what your vampire friends that you live with might do. Thirst can take control quickly."

"Okay," I said. *I don't plan on killing people. The thought of becoming a monster bothered me. I won't be one, I'll stay good.*

"Funny thing about that Alaskan town," Skip added with a smile. "Some humans think that the people disappearing are caused by alien abduction. They even made an old movie titled *The Fourth Kind*. It came out in 2009, I think."

The old vampire that I met at the bathroom door came up the steps to the roof. Now that I saw him again, he reminded me of a car mechanic —in a bad way.

"So," the old man said to Skip, "have you asked them yet?"

Skip shook his head. "No Morg, I don't think it was them."

"What, what's going on?" I asked.

"Is it possible you could live so close and not know it?" the old vampire, Morg, asked.

"All right, ask me." I twisted the cap off a bottle of beer.

"Wait," Morg said. "Are you in charge?"

"No," Lionel said. "I am."

With two beers, I was feeling grumpy, not mellow. I almost decked him. It would have to wait.

Morg continued. "We were wondering why a coven went silent in your area. That's why Madison was in the boonies yesterday. All of them were killed, a total wipe out."

"We didn't kill them," Lionel said.

"Then who did?" Morg stepped towards us, his arms crossed.

"Don't know," I said. *How am I to know?* I wasn't going to mention Robert Neville, survivor of that attack.

"Look… " Madison stood, walked up to Morg and poked him in the chest, "… they didn't do it, Morg. I asked them when I invited them here the other day."

The old man shrugged, "Alright, I believe 'em."

I doubted that.

Morg scowled and left.

Before we left, we got parting gifts. Two blood bags in an ice chest. She must have read my looks.

She pointed to one of the blood bags and said, "Tweaker blood."

Great, she thinks I like drug addicts' blood because of my lie. But the truth is, in the vampire world, I am a vegetarian or vegan. "Thanks," I said.

At the car, my anger still held for Lionel. I'd given him the cooler of blood bags and waited until he placed them in the trunk to confront him.

"What the hell was that?" I asked, my gaze boring into his eyes.

"What?" Confusion crinkled his face. Then it dawned on him what I was talking about. "Yeah, he looked like trouble, so I said I was the coven leader."

I stood inches from his face. "Never do that again. I'm in charge. You can't risk your life like that. I can't have you getting in danger."

"Well, we can't lose you," he said, heading to the driver side door. "I'll drive. You're drunk."

Fifteen minutes into the drive, I apologized, "Sorry, I felt guilty about you coming."

"You're becoming your mother," he said, keeping his gaze on the road.

"No, I'm not."

"Yes, you are."

Maybe he's right.

"They separated us on purpose," Lionel said, keeping his gaze ahead on the road while he drove.

"I noticed that. It scared me when you were gone."

"I did fine," Lionel sounded confident.

"Thanks Lionel," I said, with my head in my hand, the feeling of danger only hitting me now.

"They were weirdly less scary than I thought," Lionel said, turning the car onto the freeway.

True.

35. I AM LEGEND

"We've got company," Lionel said, from the security room.

I looked out the window as an old car drove up the road. Though no markings told of the car's organization, a single, flashing orange light flickered on the top of the vehicle. Stranger still, the driver sat in the passenger seat.

This is weird.

I stood next to the front door with my AR-15 beside me and out of sight. Everyone else hurried to their assigned positions. Even though this didn't look like an attack, we all rushed to our places, just in case. Lionel raced down the stairs and hid behind the couch, his rifle ready.

"I think it's the mail lady," Cordelia said over the walkie.

Nice, we try to hide, and we still get junk mail.

A lady exited the car with a box. *So,* she *is the letter carrier. Gosh, the guns are overkill. If the woman knew everyone inside had guns ready for her, she'd freak.*

Then I remembered, they don't have regular mail

trucks in the country. That's why she sat in the opposite seat, so she can deliver envelopes in mailboxes without leaving her car.

"Wait," I clicked transmit on the walkie. "Did anyone order anything?"

"Nope," Felix said on the radio.

No one is expecting anything.

I opened the door still feeling nervous. I knew this isn't likely an attack. Either of our parents' Houses would come up with a more direct means to our capture. She handed me a box. I thanked her, but quickly noticed that the package was addressed to no one living here. *Perhaps it's for someone who lived here when Rachel called this place home.*

I almost protested, but the mail lady made it half-way to her car when I looked up.

One object slid inside, suggesting the box to be almost empty. The content sounded like a smooth disk. *Fine, let's see what's inside.*

After the letter carrier left, we sat together opening the box. Lionel returned to the security room.

The single object in the package turned out to be a driver's license from Ohio.

"What is this?" I said, looking at the license in my hand.

Felix took the box. "Maybe the name on the

address is the real name of our Robert Neville."

"Why would you think that?" I asked, handing Felix the license.

"Because, I found the real Robert Neville." He showed me his tablet, and on the screen was an eBook titled, *I Am Legend*. The cover showed vampires clawing from the darkness.

"He gave a name of a character from the book," I said.

Cordelia clapped her hand to her mouth in apparent shock. "He knows about vampires."

"No one knows he's here, Felix, so how's anyone going to mail him anything?" I said.

Felix shrugged. "It's not logical, but let's see if Robert Neville is really this," he looked at whom the box was addressed to, "Russell Quinn."

36. THE NIGHT SIDE OF NATURE

With Felix searching to find where Robert Neville came from, I walked outside to feed. At the edge of the field, I spotted the rabbit again. Yes, *the* rabbit that bit me. *Well, except for size, they all look the same. So, maybe it's one that's the exact size, I don't know.*

I wondered if I could catch it. Sprinting, I seized the little thing and tumbled to the ground. The poor thing screamed.

"Ouch!" It bit me, again. That fur bag didn't waste any time on the second attack. The mean cotton-tailed rat struggled out of my grip, and scurried into the tree line. *Now I'm sure it was the same one.*

"Ha-ha." My sister stood on the porch with her phone out. "I was gonna snap a picture of my psycho-vampire-sister biting a rabbit. Now, I've got a picture of a rabbit biting my sister!"

Me biting a rabbit would make an awful picture. "We'll see how you handle it when you change."

"Ha, you're not setting a high bar. Now go off and kill a furry animal."

"Maybe next time I'll just stay home and bite you."

"Nah, that's what the Taser is for."

Ugh, sisters suck, no matter how dangerous you are.

A crazy idea hit me while skulking in the woods. Perhaps it's the lack of blood in my system that turns my thinking crazy. Like, just before I go out, I think of biting people in my coven. My thought may have more to do with the rabbit bite quickly healing on my finger. But the thought did not leave easily. *Is there anything dangerous in the woods?*

I understood that a dangerous animal *could* kill me. But, something in me remained a little crazy. *Is there a little blood-crazed hunter in all vampires?*

Climbing a maple tree, I used the view to see where I should go. The wind informed me that a group of creatures traveled nearby. *Not something diminutive. Its smell has a thick odor, suggesting a large size. Its scent held hints of grass, leaves, and dirt. The smell of dirt is less, suggesting these creatures didn't crawl close to the ground, like a rabbit. They stood tall like a deer or… a wolf. Let's hope for wolf.*

I don't believe my thoughts were normal.

I followed the scent until I discovered its source, a deer path. *So, prey and what I pursue used this path. The smells are old. Following where the scent went might lead me on their hunting trail. That might take hours. Maybe if I follow the scent's origin, I might find where the hunters started—their den.*

I stalked them for what might have been a quarter mile. Again, I climbed a tree only because I discovered very fresh scent, suggesting they might have a den nearby. I didn't want to be attacked by a pack. *The fight will be on my terms.*

Ring. Cordelia called and asked if they could order pizza. They'd just discovered that our area had delivery. "We have to save money," I said.

Cordelia explained that Felix started making money as an online digital assistant and wanted to celebrate.

"Okay…," I said. Cordelia had a worry. "No, I don't think the delivery guy will know to tell our families where we are. Have fun," I said. Cordelia talked some more. I looked out into the woods, seeing grey eyes glaring at me. "No. Don't save any pizza for me, I may be very full." I hung up the phone.

I heard a second wolf pad softly on the ground. Its smell thickened while it closed in, and a new scent wafted from it… fear.

I am something to be scared of? Wow.

The craving of blood rushed in my head.

I remained in control, but my mind tunneled on blood.

The first wolf stepped out of the shadows, growling. I leapt. Time slowed. I crashed toward the ground with only air rushing by me. With me still in mid-air, the wolf snapped its teeth at me. Before I landed, I punched its snout. Saliva whipped from his maw.

The second wolf dashed towards me. Its mouth opened, exposing red gums and jagged teeth. I stood. It growled. With a punch across the wolf's face, its breath gushed out on my fist.

The first returned, leaping at me with a growl. I grabbed it by the front paws and swung the animal like a baseball bat at a tree. With the first wolf's body wrapped around the tree, the second darted to me. A line of blood dangled from its mouth.

I kicked the wolf's chin, then wrestled it to the ground, snapping its neck at 180 degrees.

Except for my heart pounding, all was silent.

I yanked the creature to my mouth and bit deep. The blood warmed my body.

I stood and roared. *I am a predator.*

* * *

One mile away, Felix looked up from his phone. "Is that your sister roaring?"

Cordelia rolled her eyes. "No way, my sister can't kill a rabbit. I have video proof."

Felix's eyebrows shot up. "Okay, this I gotta see."

*   *   *

With warm wolf blood rushing through me, I didn't know how to feel at first. Blood and dirt covered my clothes. *They didn't mention that in the Twilight books.*

At home, everyone was gathered around the TV. They were streaming a movie and eating pizza.

"I'd hate to see the other guy," Lionel said, when I entered the room.

Cordelia looked concerned.

"Wolves," I said.

I sat down on the couch between Felix and my sister. A smell came from Felix. It smelled like emotion. Fear, anger, and excitement smell similar. This was neither. *I think he likes me.*

"I think I'll have some pizza, if that's okay," I said.

"Wolves you said?" Felix looked at me.

"Two. They fought."

"Wow," Felix said.

I decided I could get used to this feeding on animal thing. *That rabbit better watch out.*

37. RUSSELL QUINN

Robert Neville lay on the couch sleeping.

"How long has he been out of bed?" I asked.

"About an hour," Cordelia said. "I think he's getting better."

His face showed more color.

"Look," Felix whispered, coming close to me. He showed a picture of Robert Neville from a news article on his phone. "His name *is* Russell Quinn. So that box mailed to this house was for him. But after reading up on him, things seem to get even weirder. According to the article on our guy, this isn't the first time he disappeared."

"Great, what's going on, Felix?"

He looked at his tablet. "Russell Quinn vanished once before. A few years ago, when he was in his late teens, he disappeared for 48 hours."

I paced the living room and looked at Russell sleeping on the couch. *He lied to us about his name, but the man has been through a great ordeal. He might believe he had a reason to lie.* "Come with me. I don't want to wake him."

In the dining room, Felix continued, "Before his original disappearance, he was doing astronomy homework with a friend. His study partner drove to a gas station to get food and upon his return, he found that Russell Quinn had vanished. However, he was a part of a string of disappearances, but he was the only one found again. A pair of siblings disappeared about the time he did. Their names were Justin and Lisa Obrinski."

"Were they seen again?" I asked.

Felix shook his head. "Some people thought they saw the younger sister, Lisa Obrinski, in the woods near where Russell had vanished. But no one could track her down. Investigators assumed they were false sightings."

"When Russell was found again, did he say what happened?"

"No, Russell never said anything except that he got lost in the woods. The police didn't believe his story because he had many wounds. The authorities said his injuries were consistent with a fight. Furthermore, he turned up about the time the girl, Lisa, vanished."

"Something, likely a vampire, is making these people vanish." I looked at Felix's phone. "But why?"

Cordelia shook her head. "Unless the news article

says he had bites on him, it doesn't sound like vampires."

"What else might it be?" I shrugged.

"Remember my drawings," my sister said.

The drawings that Anne and I found. One looked like a drawing of hell. I remember a frightened girl with a trail of bloody footprints behind her. She looked over her shoulder, scared. In a burning house near her, a woman carved children's faces like a pumpkin. Flames leapt from the smiling mouths and eyes. That can't be real.

Cordelia ran upstairs. A minute later, she returned with a handful of her drawings. The one on the top was the picture of the girl. "Do you have a picture of Lisa Obrinski?" she asked Felix.

Felix nodded and scrolled his phone to a picture of Lisa Obrinski in the news article. It matched the girl in Cordelia's drawing.

I shook my head, looking at the carving woman in my sister's picture. She had a gleeful smirk while she cut a smile into the little boy's face. "What the hell is going on here?"

38. THE CALL OF MADNESS

Months ago, my sister Cordelia drew a picture of a girl who was part of a string of disappearances that included Russell Quinn. Something bad happened to him, even before I discovered him lying unconscious in the coven.

I paced the dining room, trying to figure this out. *So, he's a part of these strange disappearances. Only the girl, Lisa Obrinski, has unconfirmed sightings. Whatever the ordeal, Russell returned with only a beating. Yet, my sister who drew the future, or the past, can only draw hell when it concerns him. What does that mean? Perhaps Cordelia can't see clearly when it comes to him.*

"Cordelia, what were you thinking when you drew this?" Felix held the picture of Lisa Obrinski.

"Like I said before, I don't remember. I sort of wake up from whatever compels me to draw these things."

"Nothing?"

"Sorry, I can't be much help," Cordelia shrugged.

I looked at Russell in the living room. "I don't want you to freak, but just in case, have your Glocks ready. He might be the victim in all this, but we don't know that yet."

I returned to the news article on Felix's phone.

"Whoa," Cordelia said. I ignored her. I thought she was reading something on her tablet. "Whoa guys, look."

My gaze swung to my sister, who pointed to where Russell had lain. He had vanished from the sofa.

Lionel's voice came over our walkies. "Umm, Robert's outside at the edge of the field."

He didn't yet know that Robert wasn't his name. I radioed Lionel, "How did he get there?"

"I've no idea. I just saw him pop up there."

"Search rewind. Tell us what you see," I said.

"Yep. He just shows up," Lionel said, after a few seconds.

"What the hell is going on?" Felix followed me out to the living room.

I looked out the window. Far off near the tree line, our strange guest stood. *A minute ago, the man was too weak to stay awake. How did he get there?*

"Cordelia, show me that other picture, the one of the guy standing outside this house."

Cordelia handed me a drawing of the house burning and covered in what looked like ice. Where Russell stood and what he's wearing matches Cordelia's picture. *Our house isn't covered in ice or burning, but in other ways this is another of Cordelia's pictures proven correct. What does it all mean?*

Russell stumbled to the house.

"I'm getting answers." I dropped the picture to the floor. "He's going to tell us everything."

39. CHILDREN OF SHADOWS

The strange man, Russell Quinn, stumbled to the house, still weak. I marched out to help him. Yet, I wondered if I was assisting a danger to my family. *So much about him is strange.*

I took his arm, and wrapped it over my shoulder, allowing his weight to sink on to me. He felt warm, and a bit sweaty.

"You're not human, are you?" I asked, as we were about halfway to the house.

He took his weight off my shoulder. "They're human," he said, gesturing to Cordelia and Felix at the front door. "What are you?"

How does he know that I'm not human?

His gaze fixed on me as I backed off to four feet away.

What if my fear is correct? He's not a survivor but the killer? He killed monsters. That doesn't make him one. "I'm a vampire. My mother had me turned. I feed off deer."

That appeared to calm him. His shoulder sank. One hand rested on his knee while he stood, awkwardly stooped over.

"Look, let me help you upstairs," I said.

Once in bed, he didn't appear ready to fall asleep right away.

"Can I get you anything?" I asked.

He shook his head.

I'd decided to get answers. I believed it best to start with something simple. "What do you know about vampires?"

Russell's faced showed pain beyond his years. Not just anger but sadness cut around his eyes. "Enough to hate them."

That didn't answer much. *I hated vampires, too. And I am one.*

"Why did you survive the bites?"

"I wasn't human for a while. When I was bitten, some of what I once was came back. I guess not being fully human when bitten saved me."

"What do you mean by you weren't human for a while?"

"For forty-eight hours, I was something else."

"What happened? What were you?"

"It doesn't matter."

It does matter. I need answers, I'll try from a different angle. I brought in Cordelia's pictures. My sister waited at the threshold of Russell's room.

"Is this what happened. What does this mean?" As I asked, I showed him the horrible picture of Lisa Obrinski.

The color on his face vanished.

"What is this?" I asked.

He stared at it for a few long seconds. "Who drew it?"

I dared not look over my shoulder at my sister, but only said, "Someone very special to me. They can draw the future and the past, but when it comes to you, things get weird."

"She hasn't been there?" Russell asked.

"This is real?"

His eyes narrowed and his gaze lowered.

"What does the picture mean? Are we in any danger?"

"No."

"Liar!" I grabbed the picture of Lisa Obrinski in that hellish place and shoved it close to his face. "This woman is carving into the face of a boy. Why is this little girl Lisa in the middle of it?"

He looked me in the eye, his tone not showing any agitation. He must have practiced being under pressure. "She was there, but none of that actually happened. We see people's souls through the eyes of God."

I sat down. "That's a riddle, not an answer." But that still told me more than he might have intended. The word "they" means there are more than one of whatever he is. And they likely informed him of whatever this place was. "So this place is…?"

"It's like dreams come alive. It's a time when we don't see the outside of people, but what is within. I can't tell you more."

"Why not?"

"You hate your kind, I know. If you were to reveal things, my people would be in danger. The less your people know, the better."

"Okay, what about this license we got in the mail."

He closed his eyes and looked away with a sigh. "A long time ago, I should have killed someone very bad. I didn't. So, I am reminded of my mistake with every driver's license sent to me. With each person who dies, I get a license."

"The killer knows your address? *Our* address?"

"Something stranger than the both of us is angry at me for letting a boy live—a very evil boy." He turned away in bed.

I left him to rest after that. *I got answers, but things make even less sense in some ways.*

A man who walks dreams? Claims to see through the eyes of God? Who survived vampire bites because he wasn't fully human? He's likely a little crazy. Russell isn't much older than me, but he's been through a lot. No wonder he's lost his sanity.

But how do I explain his teleporting outside?

Felix met me at the door. "I just read up on Russell's second disappearance, which happened a few weeks ago. His wife disappeared first, and then his daughter." Felix followed me down the stairs. "When you discovered Russell, didn't you say a small vampire girl led him to the coven?"

He didn't need to ask that. I'd already put together a strange picture. *That girl may have been his daughter. He wasn't being lured into a trap. He was out for revenge. That's why she didn't go to the house, but instead waited at the tree line. She watched her father fight for his life.*

No, that makes no sense. No one survives a fight six to one.

Then a thought came to me. *The mother vanished,*

then the daughter. He wasn't just going after strange vampires. Did he want to kill his wife for turning their daughter?

What have I gotten in to?

40. A MAN NAMED MORGAN

Jonathan looked nervous as he whispered to me, "Anne, can we trust these people?"

"I don't. But, Fiona is going to kill me if I don't find Alexia. She keeps her promises. Well… she keeps the bad ones, anyway."

This was a group of working class vampires. Olympia had a large scene of our kind because they could enjoy the city while going out to the country to hunt. These vampires fit in with humans. But Morg had gathered these dozen people because they had one hook that could pull all of them, greed.

"How is the pot to be divided?" one of the vampires asked.

I tell them firmly, but slowly, "I don't care. I'm giving the money to Morg. You guys figure that out yourselves."

"I'm leading this, so I get 10%," Morg said. "The other 90% will be divided evenly."

People seemed to be okay with that.

"What about weapons?" A female vampire asked.

"You'll have them. Morg will supply you, but you shouldn't need them. They are expected to come peacefully. This is an extraction."

"If this is easy, then why the numbers? Why the sum of money?" Another vampire I believed to be named Skeeter asked.

"House matters, don't ask questions," I said.

There was a chuckle at that. I'd seen people online making fun of statements like I'd just made. But no one followed up the question.

"Everyone get ready. We go now," Morg said. He walked up to me while the others marched out. "Your friend Madison is going to hate you for this."

"That's why you're being paid not to say anything."

Morg smiled. His eyes gleamed with a weird humor.

As long as he got the job done, I'll live.

41. BLOOD RAIL

"There are easier ways of getting a divorce," Lionel said, catching a Frisbee.

Felix and I gasped. "Lionel, that's horrible."

I explained my theory that Russell Quinn attacked the coven seeking revenge, and may have killed his wife for turning their daughter.

"Yeah it's messed up, but things are so awful, we may as well laugh at them," Lionel added, throwing the disk my way. "That doesn't explain the driver's license."

Lionel referred to the driver's license that the mail lady brought in a box. We discovered Russell Quinn's real name on the package that was addressed to him.

I tossed the Frisbee to Felix. "You tell him." Felix had already told me.

"Yeah, the person on the driver's license died the

day we got the package in the mail. The box came from Ohio. That person is believed to be part of a string of murders that happened the night Russell Quinn reappeared, and the little girl vanished."

Lionel frowned, catching the Frisbee from Felix. "This guy isn't safe."

"Vampires attacked him, Lionel. We are the dangerous ones," I said.

"Everything about him is about death. Vampires die. A string of deaths starts years ago when he reappears. He's bad news." Lionel threw the Frisbee to me.

I caught it. He had a point. I didn't mention that Russell Quinn had said that the driver's licenses are sent as a reminder of his failure to kill this killer. That sounded too crazy.

Lionel shook his head. "If he goes crazy on you guys, I'm offing him."

"If he attacks, very well. But only then," I said.

"The next time he wakes up, he's telling us how he teleported," Lionel said.

"He didn't teleport, look," Felix said, gesturing for the two of us to follow. We both walked to where he stood. Felix pointed to a part in the grass where Russell had stood last night. The grass looked like it had been beaten down. "I watched the video that showed him suddenly appearing at this spot. When he appears to teleport in the video, there is a blur in the area he appears for a fraction of a second. I don't think it was like teleporting to him. Time just slowed for us and continued to seem normal for him. It looks like he paced back and forth for a while, waiting for time to become normal."

The grass did appear well trampled on. Teleporting or time-slowing were both absurd ideas. But I'd no idea what to believe. "We don't know what's going on. We'll ask him when he gets up."

It's odd. I am a vampire, and yet there is still something weirder and stranger than me.

42. THE DEAD ARE COMING ...

Russell stumbled down the stairs and staggered to the window. "Everyone stay inside."

"What's wrong?" I asked.

Everyone turned to him.

"The dead…." he didn't say anything for a moment. "Their bloods cries out. I hear them. They're in the woods. They are hiding behind the trees."

Lionel shook his head. "He's lost it."

He said their blood cries out. If people could hear blood cry out, it could be vampires.

"Three cars are driving up the gravel road," Felix said from the security room.

Three cars? What is this?

I looked outside and saw a trio of vehicles driving in the dim light.

My phone vibrated in my pocket. My heart stopped when I saw Anne's number was calling. How did she get this number?

"Hello?" My throat dried as I said the words.

Anne's voice sounded even. "I have to get you, or your mother will kill me. Tell everyone they are coming with me."

Then she hung up.

43. IT BEGINS ...

"I'm going out," I said.

Everyone looked surprised, even Russell Quinn.

"When I go, I'll say that I need to talk you guys into leaving. That'll buy you time. Get your weapons."

Lionel shook his head. "They found us. They'll find us again."

"No, they'll kill us here," Cordelia said.

Lionel's gaze dropped to the floor. "I'm just saying—"

Russell spoke, "I've killed a whole bunch of vampires before. You'll see me do it again. Go, outside. We'll cover for you."

I felt vulnerable when I stepped outside. While I walked into the field where the car had driven on the grass,

I knew that any one of them could shoot me. Others hid among the trees. *All it takes is one shot and I'd turn ravenous and dart back into the house and hurt my sister or the brothers.*

I looked ahead. Russell said there were people in the woods. He's correct; I heard them, though they remained silent and hidden, as if ready to attack if things went wrong. I saw three people beside a black Chevy. The car's fender had something to help it ram into things. Three people stood by the car: Anne, my former friend; Morg, who, no doubt, narc'd us out, and a third. My heart missed a beat. Jonathan.

His eyes were cold. Anger hardened the look in his eyes that didn't blink or turn away from me. His features were porcelain. He looked like a Greek statue of a young man that had come to life.

"Jonathan," I gasped. *This is your fault. This is your fault.* Then I managed, "How?"

"You sold me out. Left me behind. I deserve better." His normally calm features twisted with pent-up rage. *He's angry at me.*

The cold eyes narrowed, he came close, "Why didn't you tell me, Alexia?"

"I didn't want this. I didn't think she would do anything to you." He was right; he *did* deserve better, and I had left him behind. I'd no idea Mother would do such a thing. "Jonathan, I can make this right," I said.

Anne said, "You can make this right by

surrendering. You will be treated well."

Morg made an exaggerated bow. "Come with us, my Princess."

When he'd finished his mock bow, I kicked him in the crotch. The man plunked onto all fours. Even as a vampire, they still hurt a lot, and that wasn't a normal girl kick. No, that was a strong vampire kick.

Everyone's weapon pointed at me.

"What are you going to do?" I asked everyone. "I am royalty, after all."

"This is serious," Anne said. "Get them out here and things will be fine. Don't you make us wait, either.

"I will get my fam—coven," I said with disdain as I strutted away. Just before I turned, I noted a skeptical look from my former friend, Anne.

The walk back might only take second, but for me it took forever. I felt fear crush my heart and stomach. The question lingered, is this all for nothing? It's one thing to be brave in theory, but another to actually do something brave. Fear ran through me. Only yesterday, I was predator. Now, I was prey. *No, stop thinking like that. I have to protect my sister, Felix, and Lionel.*

I looked to Russell, "Yes, you were right, there are more people in the woods." I looked to Felix and Cordelia. "Just like we practiced, go upstairs, and be ready to fire. And oh, Cordelia, try and spot people in the woods. Get them before they break the tree line, if you can. Felix, if she shoots someone, make sure they don't run to the house. Spray them with three shots. They'll be coming for you."

"Got it," he said.

"Ten seconds," Morg yelled on a bullhorn.

"Russell, this is not your fight," I said, knowing I didn't want to lose him. *We need all the help we can get.*

He looked sad. "I failed as a father, and as a husband. I won't let myself fail as a friend. That's all I have left."

That was the saddest and most noble thing I had ever heard. "You did not fail your family."

"Five seconds," Morg yelled.

"I stay," Russell said.

Great. How good can I be that I am having someone risk his life for us when he doesn't have a real stake in this? "Everyone, you know what to do," I said.

Everyone dashed into their positions. Doubt sunk in. *No, I'm not letting Mom have my sister.*

To Russell, I said, "Here's a Glock."

Russell shook his head. "I can't use them. We bond to metallic objects, so firing a gun can be discombobulating. Trust me."

What does that mean? "Then what will you do?"

"Ka-Bar?"

I gave him a Ka-Bar, a military knife, more like a dagger.

He frowned taking it. Rubbing his shoulder.

"Better start coming out now!" Morg yelled.

I moved behind the couch.

In the dark, I saw better than most humans. I looked at Morg standing in the sunroof of the car, yelling something about coming to get us. I made sure my aim was good. From behind the living room couch, I made the first shot of the battle. I pulled the trigger, and he sunk into the sunroof of his car like a rock.

It has begun.

44. SIEGE

I heard the sound of glass smashing. It came from our garage. Everything went black. They'd cut the circuit breaker.

"Damn it, I'll get them," Lionel said, offering to shoot those who killed the lights.

"No, I'll go," Russell offered.

"You watch her back," he pointed to me. "I got this," Lionel said to Russell, and ran into the darkness.

"You want a fight," Morgan yelled through a bullhorn. "You have one."

An engine roared, and grew louder, racing toward the house. I fired at the car aiming for the driver. The sound of gunfire upstairs told me Felix and my sister were trying to stop it, too.

What's their game charging the house?

Crash!

The front door and window on our left caved in. The car stopped with the front door laying on the cracked windshield. No air bags.

Morgan cursed. "Get out. Get out."

Charging the house was stupid.

I pointed my iron sights at the driver, whom I recognized from Madison's coven, Slick.

Bam! Blood splattered all over the window.

Morg stumbled out of the backseat. After stepping out of the car, he fired his shotgun twice. Both shots missed, taking chunks out of the sofa.

Russell dragged me into the dining room.

Felix felt the house shake when the car crashed into the house.

I hope everyone down there is okay, Felix thought.

Bam! Cordelia fired.

Felix's eyes raced, trying to find who she shot. Two of the cars remained in the front yard. His eyes stopped on a man yanking a driver out of the front seat. *Cordelia may have made a mistake by shooting the drivers; the other vampires aren't trying to ram the house like Morg did. They may just want to get out of here at this point. They aren't up for a fight.*

Instead of easy money, they're getting hammered.

One vampire knelt at the rear of a car. It looked like he took aim at the second floor. Felix fired, missing several times until one spun the vampire to the ground.

Felix assessed the whole fight. Two driver's seats covered in shattered glass and blood. *Great, Morg's stupid charge doomed everyone. Now every driver seat is a target and no one can retreat. That increases the number of ravenous vampires running toward us.*

Some of the vampires fired at the house, even while others smartly dashed for the forest.

With each shot Cordelia fired, a vampire fell, and she aimed at the next target. But Felix spotted that some rose up. He tried shooting a few before they make it to the house. *They aren't thinking. They are blood crazed.* Felix shuddered, recalling Alexia when she was shot on their first attempt to escape.

A furious scream emanated from the living room. Russell and I were alone in the hallway. I waited down the hall, gun pointed and ready to fire.

"Alexia," Russell said to me. He stood at the bathroom threshold. Gesturing for me to follow. Russell waited with his Ka-Bar just inside.

Careful to have my gun pointed down the hall, I stood at the threshold at Russell's suggestion. *What if I get shot and bleed out so much that I become ravenous and try to kill my sister and Felix? Can't think about that now. I should have given Russell a gun. He's crazy, but he can use a gun regardless of what he said. I need him to be able to shoot others.*

Russell gasped, "Screamers are running to the house."

Bam! Bam! Bam!

"Never mind," Russell said.

What are screamers? He must mean ravenous. "What is Morg waiting for?" I asked, hearing more gunfire.

"More screamers are coming for us," Russell warned.

Morg must be waiting for the others to charge the house. He's wised up after that stupid stunt with the car.

Paper white, bleeding vampires dart down the hall. They're ravenous. Even in the dark, their faces look twisted with pangs of thirst. *That's what I looked like after being shot.* I fired, taking more down. Yet another group of vampires trampled over the fallen as they charged down the hallway. *How many have Cordelia and Felix shot and made ravenous?*

We lock ourselves in the bathroom.

Bam! The door throbbed on impact.

45. UPSTAIRS SHOOTING GALLERY

"Stop firing," Felix yelled.

"What?" Cordelia looked perplexed.

"Let them run away. They're darting to the house, ravenous. I can't get them all."

"Oh."

Bam! Something hit the door.

Felix felt relieved he'd locked the door. He Unleashed three shots through it, then three more. Vampires broke the door, growling in the near pitch black. Cordelia swung her gun at the doorway and fired two shots.

"I got 'em, Felix," Cordelia said.

"Thanks," Felix said, "I'll watch the door."

46. TOOTH AND SHOTGUN

A light fixture shed a shaft of weak evening light into the otherwise dark bathroom. The electricity was still out, only dim sunlight came through. Russell signaled me not to fire at the door. Instead, he thrust the Ka-Bar into the wood. A woman on the other side let out a primal scream.

Morg cursed outside the bathroom.

Boom!

A basketball-sized hole burst through the door. The blast narrowly missed Russell. A shotgun pellet nicked me. White arms sprouted from the hole. They reached for Russell. I fired at the hands. A pair of the arms zipped into the black hole, another went limp.

"Damn it!" Morg yelled. I heard what must be his feet pounding away down the hall, apparently retreating.

A bleeding pair of white arms reached through the hole. Russell yanked an arm up and did something strange. He bit down on the pale white hand. From Russell's skin gushed white mist over a few of the bites that lined his arms. The wounds vanished in a flash. He chucked the pale arm down, and it fell limp next to the other arms that I shot. The pair of ravenous vampires, now dead. *That's how he killed all the vampires in the coven, he's a vampire of vampires.*

"Run," I said. I dived for the bathroom's back door, firing three shots through it before yanking it open.

Morg stood bleeding at the threshold, with anger burning in his eyes. His shotgun clicked, firing nothing. Then he cracked his shotgun across my face.

I plunked onto the floor.

Morg towered over me, popping the spent shells out and reloading.

Russell charged Morg, sliding the blade into his ample belly. His white shirt gushed red. Unleashing a primal scream, the vampire aimed the shotgun at Russell's face. Twisting the blade, Russell gripped the barrel with his other hand vying for control of the gun. Morg's eyes beamed hatred. The vampire stumbled back as Russell shoved his shoulder into the barrel. The Ka-Bar remained at the hilt in Morg's stomach, slicing towards his chest.

I stood and aimed my gun, but Russell blocked my shot.

Bam! Morg's shotgun fired. The vampire's face erupted, becoming a mask, dripping of blood and meat.

Morg let out a battle cry, spitting red droplets. He bit down on Russell's shoulder. They both fell to the ground. My friend yanked at the vampire's jaw by the teeth, prying the biting mouth open. Morg's cheeks stretched as Russell continued to pull. A morbid clicks, then a crack. Morg's jaw ripped free from his face. Russell pounded the jaw on the ravenous vampire's head. My poor friend's face twisted in rage. *He's not just pounding the vampire. He's beating those who turned his family, raging at the fate of his daughter, his wife, his own fate.*

"It's done, Russell. It's done," I said.

He dropped the jaw on the smoking shotgun. "I know."

47. AFTERMATH

After Russell beat Morg to death, everything hushed. I heard whispers of my sister and Felix upstairs. We all seemed to wait for more gunfire, but none thundered.

Russell stared at nothing, still in a world of his own, kneeling over Morg's body.

"Cordelia, are you okay?" I asked into my walkie.

"Thank God, you're alive, Alexia. Both Felix and I are fine."

"You're not hurt?" I asked.

"We're okay. They busted through the door," Felix said. "But we got 'em."

"Stay where you are, guys. I'm going to check if everything's okay." Then to Russell, "Wait here."

From the bathroom, I heard no sounds in the

house, but for a breeze, yet I worried someone hid anyway.

I peeked out the bathroom, careful not to make a sound. Every corner held danger, so I kept my eyes glued down the hall. But the house remained still. I stepped into the living room. Only the curtains rippled with the breeze.

Behind me someone moved. I turned 180 degrees, pointing my gun in that direction. He thrust his hands up.

Russell spoke, "Only the wounded out in the yard remain."

"Damn it, Russell. I might have shot you," I said, and lowered my gun. "How do you know who remains? You only just left the bathroom."

"The blood they stole is not silent, it screams for me to avenge them."

Crazy, what the hell does that even mean? "Go back to the bathroom."

Ignoring my words, he said, "You mentioned Madison was your friend." Russell handed me a phone. "You should see this, the ugly guy I just killed received a text."

"You mean, Morg?" I asked.

He shrugged and showed me Morg's phone.

Maddie: Traitor!

Maddie: You are not coming back to my coven.

All these texts happened during battle. I realized "Maddie" must be Madison.

A morbid thought crossed my mind; I considered taking a selfie with dead Morgan in the background to offer proof to Madison that I was okay, but I figured a mutilated dead vampire was in bad taste. *Still, I'd like to see Mom's face if I posted that selfie with a note on social media: Thanks Mom, for teaching me everything I needed to know.*

The thought felt oddly amusing.

I texted back on Morgan's phone.

Me: Madison, it's Alexia. Don't worry, all the traitors are dead. We are fine.

Madison: I'm glad you're okay.

Still wary of shooters, I continued to search the living room, but with my vampire hearing I felt it unlikely there were any. My gun pointed at the car that had rammed our front door. The back driver's side door hung open, both seats empty. With Russell next to me, I opened the driver's door. Slick, the punk that was too high to be awake when I visited Madison's coven, stared at me, dead.

After I checked the first floor, Lionel came out of the garage and said, "Our car has a few bullet holes, but I believe it should work."

I told him we'd test it soon, relieved that he was okay.

Felix stumbled down the stairs first, then Cordelia.

They walked over to the car that crashed by the stairs. As Cordelia gave me a hug, her rifle slung over her shoulder, her gun barrel touched my skin.

"Ouch. Your gun's still sizzling hot," I said. She apologized, but I didn't care, she was fine.

The others looked at Russell, his shirt covered in blood.

"You okay?" Cordelia asked.

He nodded, "Most of it's not mine."

I looked to the bathroom door where both of us had left bloody footprints. "Yeah, if you need to go to the bathroom, let us take the body out."

Lionel's eyebrows perked up, and he went to the door. I warned him, but he opened the door anyway.

His hand clasped to his mouth. "Wow, Russell, glad you're on our side."

I looked through the shattered windows, a handful of bodies crawled in the grass making their way to our house. *None in the house, a few wounded outside, just like Russell Quinn said.*

"They smell us, the humans, that is," Lionel said, looking through the shattered windows.

"I'll go out there," I said. Killing those already fallen turned my stomach, yet I'd no choice. I knew we needed to leave our house, but if we left the crawling, blood-crazed vampires here, they'd crawl until they found a human.

"There might still be snipers at the edge of the woods," Lionel said.

That received nods from Felix and Cordelia.

"There aren't," Russell insisted. "I would be able to tell if anyone was within about a quarter mile."

That still sounds crazy. I said to the others, "Anyone who hasn't fought yet likely ran. They were marauders, not real fighters. We didn't kill them, so much as their over-confidence killed them. Plus, I can see better than humans in the dark. If there is anyone at the edge of the woods, I'll spot them."

"But, we can shoot them from here!" Cordelia said.

"No, don't waste your ammo." I didn't worry about bullets. I worried for Jonathan and Anne, possibly laying wounded on the battlefield. *If I can save them I will.*

"I'll go with you," Russell said.

I nodded. Yet, worried what he might do.

The two of us exited the front door, telling the others to cover us. I passed a dead vampire. All of those times Cordelia had shot tea jugs from the second story window had paid off.

I crossed another dead vampire; several of the

bullet wounds appeared smaller than Cordelia's rounds. I knew it to be Felix's work. "Good boy." *He probably doesn't want me calling him a boy, especially, if he likes me.*

Russell Quinn yanked up a ravenous vampire; the wounded creature cried out in pain.

"No, that's Jonathan." I ran to Russell and my ex-boyfriend, his skin white as a cloud. Both his eyes were wide open and oddly blank. No thought in them.

Jonathan mechanically snapped his teeth at Russell's hand, inches out of reach.

"I'll get him blood." First, I scanned the field, looking to see if Anne lie wounded, too. But the other two were men I didn't recognize. Both inched on their stomachs toward Russell. If he worried they might harm him, he didn't show it. *One of the three cars is now gone. Anne must have bolted during the battle.* "Finish off the rest of them," I said, darting to the house.

Russell plunked my ex to the ground. "With pleasure."

I returned, glad I still had a blood bag from Madison's coven. Jonathan drank greedily. His complexion returned, but he remained speechless. He looked at me, his face hard to read.

Jonathan, don't hate me. "You're going to be fine," I told him.

Jonathan looked at me, still expressionless.

Russell buried the bodies. I felt grateful to him for taking on the ghastly task.

We gathered in the car, but I didn't know where we were going to go. We survived Mom's first attack on us. By a miracle, none of us were seriously hurt.

Driving away from our home, I spotted someone at the edge of the woods in the rear view mirror. At first, I thought it might be one of our attackers, but the figure was too small, perhaps a little girl. A second later, the person vanished.

To be continued…

ABOUT THE AUTHOR

Although my mother is English, and I was born in Scotland, I've spent little time in the British Isles. I've lived much of my life in and around the Pacific—be it Hawaii, Guam, Japan or the West Coast of the United States.

Visit my website and subscribe to my newsletter at, jameskpratt.com

ALSO BY THE AUTHOR

Russell Quinn loses his humanity after a violent encounter with a stranger and becomes a jinn. Now the thoughts of normal people barrage his mind, making a return home impossible. Soon, Russell meets someone like him, and along the way he learns that the key to regaining his humanity is in a place called the Bend. There, one can see through the eyes of God. But even if he regains his humanity, what he glimpsed in the Bend will change the way he views himself, and others, forever.

Children of Nod is a modern dark fantasy story. It combines elements of Dante's Inferno with a flare of modern fantasy. As one critic said, *"Pratt is proving to be a highly imaginative author… a tale that is unique and original."*
S. Randall.

ALSO BY THE AUTHOR

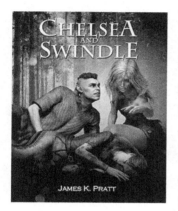

Tuk, a young goblin, witnesses the massacre of his family at the hands of greedy adventurers. Now, on a hopeless quest for vengeance, he leaves his childhood behind. His quest for justice leads him to a city ruled by humans and elves where the adventurers are seen as heroes. Along the way, he befriends two orphans like him, Chelsea and Swindle. Tuk will challenge the ruling class and awaken the goblins and orcs, who identify with him, thrusting the city to the boiling point.

Made in the USA
Monee, IL
12 September 2022